Taming the Texas Cowboy

Taming the Texas Cowboy
A Forever Texan Romance

Charlene Sands

TULE
PUBLISHING

Taming the Texas Cowboy
Copyright © 2003 Charlene Sands
Tule Publishing First Printing, January 2017

The Tule Publishing Group, LLC

ALL RIGHTS RESERVED

First Publication by Tule Publishing Group 2017
Second Edition

This book was previously titled The Cowboy Contract

No part of this book may be used or reproduced in any manner whatsoever without written permission except in the case of brief quotations embodied in critical articles and reviews.

This is a work of fiction. Names, characters, places, and incidents are products of the author's imagination or are used fictitiously. Any resemblance to actual events, locales, organizations, or persons, living or dead, is entirely coincidental.

ISBN: 978-1-945879-95-1

Chapter One

"I DO," TREY Walker uttered.

In a million lifetimes, he never dreamed he'd say these words. Especially not to Maddie Brooks, the auburn-haired beauty standing beside him, her eyes wide with gratitude. They stood under an arbor of lush traveling vines in the small garden area behind his house at 2 Hope Ranch.

"I do, too," she offered. A gentle breeze blew by and tousled her hair all sexy-like.

Trey swallowed. He was intrigued by the young woman who'd be living with him for an unforeseen length of time. In truth, the petite, green-eyed female scared the hell out of him with her innocent looks and wholesome demeanor. She was the exact sort of woman Trey avoided—the kind that said "KEEPER" in big, bold capital letters. But damn it all, if Trey hadn't needed her, or rather if 2 Hope Ranch hadn't needed what she had to offer, Trey would never have agreed to this.

"So you agree to the terms?" She repeated softly, her voice a mere whisper on the wind.

"I do, Maddie. There's no need to sign a contract. My

word is as good as gold."

Maddie nodded a bit tentatively as she swiveled her body around, glancing at his property, her slender hands set in the back pockets of her denim jeans. Trey looked his fill, enjoying the view of a perfectly formed backside. He was one to appreciate a good-looking woman and Maddie was all that—even in her range-dusty work clothes.

When she turned around, Trey snapped his head up to meet her gaze. Again, her words were soft as morning dew and Trey got the feeling she was as reluctant about this arrangement as he was. "I'll move my things in tonight, and tomorrow I'll set up my office in the old barn. The animals all seem to be doing fine. I think this might just work out."

Trey squeezed his eyes shut momentarily. He grunted a reply and held out his hand. A handshake in this part of Texas was more than enough to bind an agreement. Maddie lifted her right hand from her pocket and slid her palm into his. He shook the hand quickly before the impact of her touch could register to any other part of his body, other than his addled brain. "It's a deal then."

She bit down on her lip drawing his attention to a heart-shaped mouth so pink and ripe that Trey was certain the Almighty had made her lips expressly for kissing. Too bad, Trey thought with regret, because he'd already set Maddie Brooks strictly off-limits. She was now a business partner, of sorts.

She would rent out one room in his house, use the old

barn as her office and treat her animal patients there. Not only would 2 Hope Ranch gain from the rental fee, but Maddie had also agreed to treat all of Trey's livestock for free. It was a deal he couldn't refuse. His ranch had encountered more than a few setbacks lately, and Trey just plain needed the revenue. He'd had no choice really and neither had Maddie. Her veterinary office had burned clear down to the ground just days ago, and Trey's was the only ranch within miles that had an extra barn and a ranch house big enough to accommodate her without any problem. There was no denying Trey had plenty of room on the grounds as well as three empty bedrooms inside his house.

Trey had taken in her animals first thing after they'd been rescued by the fire department in Hope Wells. They included a yellow Labrador retriever recovering from a birdshot wound, a border collie named Toby that had been hit by a car, and two rabbits suffering from ear mites. They and various other small pets were now housed inside Trey's smaller, older barn. Hell, he couldn't have the animals suffer. They needed a home, but he hadn't bargained on Maddie coming to live with him. No sir.

Uncle Monty had pulled a fast one talking him into this arrangement, and Trey wasn't at all certain his uncle hadn't had matchmaking on his mind.

Maddie graced him with a small smile. "Deal."

Trey began to walk off but turned when a thought struck. "You need help moving your stuff in?"

"Uh, no. Not really. I don't have much at the motel but some clothes and a few things I managed to accumulate since the fire. I'm pretty much starting out fresh. I don't even have much left in the way of files." She shrugged, keeping up a brave front, but Trey figured Maddie was as broken up inside as that old border collie. "Guess I'm just going to have to improvise."

Trey nodded. Maddie lived in a small apartment above her office in town, and now she'd lost almost everything. The insurance company came through with a small sum for the time being, but the rest of her claim was contingent upon an investigation into the cause of the fire.

He tipped his hat. "I'll be here, if you need me."

He was just being neighborly, doing the polite thing, yet those words sent his body into small shock. He shuddered and turned to walk away before Maddie noticed. No sense worrying the girl. She had enough to worry over. But the fact remained that Trey didn't want to be needed.

Ever—and especially by a female.

He'd been cursed in that regard. Both his father and grandfather had bad track records when it came to women. They'd done a great job of breaking hearts and wrecking lives. Trey had seen the destruction firsthand and it hadn't been pretty. From early on, after one failed engagement, Trey had vowed to keep his own life simple. And women close only when they both agreed on temporary. Trey didn't do permanent. Nothing was going to change that.

And now that pretty little filly Maddie Brooks would be sharing bath towels with him under his roof. An image instantly flashed—Maddie's petite body wrapped in a two-by-nothing towel and bumping into him in the hallway. He paused, letting the image sink in of soft ripe curves and healthy, tanned skin all tucked into a tight little package. He caught himself and cursed up a blue streak then kicked up his heels so fast that his boots cut a straight-arrow path back to the corral.

Sometimes, being neighborly came with too high a price.

MADDIE SLOWED HER truck to a stop by the rubble that was once her home, her office and her very existence in Hope Wells. It was all gone. She'd lost the small place on the edge of town she'd proudly called home for the past year and a half. Sucking up courage, she glanced at the devastation through the truck's window. Large cinders still radiated heat and practically everything she'd owned was diminished to varying shades of black, charred beyond recognition.

Maddie stepped down from the truck and breathed in the smell of destruction. She coughed, choking on a deadly combination of burnt belongings and wafting smoke. Only a small broken-down remnant of her storefront sign remained. The sign that had once said, The Animal Place, *T.A.P. Gently*, Madeline M. Brooks, D.V.M., now only touted the first three letters of her first name, Mad. How appropriate. A little irony of life, she thought sadly. Tears welled in her eyes as she stared at the loss.

Goodness, she still didn't understand how the fire started exactly. Faulty wiring, one firefighter guessed. He'd known old Dr. Benning for years, the man who had sold Maddie his veterinary practice before moving to Dallas to be closer to his grandchildren. He'd been a mainstay in the community, a man who cared for animals until his eyesight had just about given out. Maddie, fresh out of an internship in northern California had been overjoyed at the prospect of buying a small but fully established practice and had just enough funds to cover a down payment on the asking price.

Doc Benning had stayed on for one month after the sale, guiding Maddie, introducing her to his clients, and mentoring her much like a tutor would a new student. Maddie had been grateful for the help, but she'd been eager to get started on her own. She'd studied hard, learned fast and her love of animals came easily. She'd been graced with the "touch" from a young age, a special way she had of communicating with animals that went beyond description. Her well-honed instincts—in combination with her schooled training—served her well, and Maddie was extremely proud of her accomplishments.

She reached into the truck, grabbing a beat-up pair of leather work gloves and tiptoed her way through the charred remains. Heat curled her toes from inside her boots, but it wasn't unbearable, so she ventured forth, searching. This would be the last chance she'd have to find something, anything left partially intact, before a crew would come to clear it all away. She'd been through the place once already, right after the fire. At that time she'd been too distraught to really see anything beyond the damage.

Maddie tiptoed carefully through the wreckage, her gaze traveling along slowly, eyeing each inch of ground carefully in hopes of finding something she might recognize, but nothing appeared salvageable. She sighed and turned to leave. She shouldn't have come. The venture was as fruitless as it was painful. Everything was gone.

But then a glint of something shiny caught her eye. Afternoon sunlight beamed down and at first Maddie thought it was just light reflecting off burnt metal. She stepped closer and bent to make a better inspection, putting on her gloves. With nimble fingers, she parted the ashes that partially covered her discovery. The Appaloosa emerged, a sterling-silver necklace given to her by her Grandma Mae when Maddie had graduated high school. Maddie lifted the piece, picking it up by the chain, dangling the necklace before her eyes. She gasped her relief then chuckled with glee. "Hello, Aphrodite. I should've known nothing would keep you down."

The charm appeared undamaged, except for a layer of ash that Maddie quickly blew away with a forceful gush of air. Then with a gentle rub of her gloved thumb the sterling horse winked back with luster, appearing unscathed and good as new. Clutching the charm to her chest, tears stung her eyes—tears of relief, happiness, and gratitude.

If there was one thing Maddie would have chosen to salvage from all this destruction, it would have been Aphrodite. Lucky her. Maddie believed that small miracles happened every day, and today she'd been graced with a precious one.

Grandma Mae's sage words flashed through her mind as she recalled that cloudless spring day when she'd been given the family heirloom. "Love who you are, child. Love what you do. Love your family and friends and God's creatures, and then love will also find you."

"I'm glad I found you."

Trey Walker's deep voice startled her out of her thoughts. Maddie whirled around. With her heart in her throat, she peered at him as he stood with arms folded, leaning against the cab of her truck. Trey's voice did things to her. His impossible good looks knotted her stomach. His long lean stature, that cowboy stance, the hypnotic way a tic worked at his jaw, all conspired to throw Maddie's once nicely orchestrated world upside down.

At one time, she had thought to be in love with him. She'd hoped to gain his attention since the first time she'd laid eyes on him, out in his barn at 2 Hope.

Trey had called Doc Benning out to see to an aging mare. The old girl had been failing for quite some time and Doc had brought Maddie along with him to mentor her and give her a grain of experience. She doubted she'd ever forget the image of Trey Walker bent over that old roan, whispering soft soothing words in her ear. Strong, work-roughened hands slid gently and with masterful grace over the horse's muzzle. He worked his hands along her mane, each stroke careful, calculated to give the old girl peace.

There wasn't anything she or Doc Benning could do, but give the horse a shot to put her down. But Trey disagreed. He wanted her to go as God intended, *when* He intended. And Maddie knew, without a doubt, that Trey had made the right choice. The horse had eased out of the world with Trey's loving hands caressing her softly, spilling words from his heart and speaking a final farewell to a longtime friend.

Maddie had fallen in love with Trey Walker that day—instantly and without a doubt in her mind.

But she'd been clearly disappointed when Trey Walker ignored her every attempt to gain his affection. Oh, he'd been polite, sweet as peach pie when she'd come out to check on his livestock. But he'd also been distant and at times, indifferent. Maddie had even tried a supreme makeover once—highlighting her hair, learning to do her makeup without smearing herself all up and wearing the most revealing, cleavage-spilling clothes a woman dared to wear. Nothing had worked. He hadn't given her the slightest glimmer of hope. Clearly he wanted no part of her. And seeing him around town making easy conversation with women at times surely broke her heart.

Heck, you don't have to hit Maddie Brooks over the head with a sledgehammer. She'd finally gotten the message. She'd given up. Wholly and completely.

But darn if the man standing right in front of her still didn't make her legs go wobbly. Only now, Maddie was smarter. She armed herself with steely resolve. She didn't have a clue about enticing a man like Trey. She wasn't the sort of woman to catch Trey Walker's attention. She understood that now.

"Trey, are you looking for me?"

Trey glanced at her tear-smudged face but Maddie refused to let it bother her. She wasn't out to impress Trey Walker anymore. She wouldn't rub her cheeks dry, but they burned hot as Trey's deep blue eyes studied her.

He pushed away from the truck and stood at the edge of the ashes, his gaze holding hers. "Ah, Maddie, you're crying."

Maddie stiffened her shoulders against Trey's knowing eyes. She lifted the necklace and swung it out, catching his attention. "Happy tears. I found something... something that wasn't destroyed. Something... precious."

Trey glanced at the necklace then arched a brow, but nodded in understanding.

"My grandmother gave this to me when I graduated high school. I wore it every day in college. It has special meaning."

Trey stepped into the rubble, coming up close for a better look. He reached for the necklace, his fingers brushing over her gloved hand. Even through thick leather, Maddie felt the shock of his slight touch. The careful way he lifted the jewel from her, as if he trusted that it was indeed precious, only magnified the sensation. She stared at the dark fringes of his eyelashes as he peered down and she noted a tiny quirk of a smile erupting. "It's nice. I'm glad you found it in all this mess."

Maddie glanced around. "Yes. It's about all I found." When she turned to him again, she wondered if he purposely sought her out. "What are you doing here? Do you want me for something?"

Trey pursed his lips, disguising a devil-made grin. Hell, he'd never seen anything like it. Maddie Brooks, traipsing through these ruins, with her auburn hair tangled around her face and tearstains running a path down her ash-smudged cheeks. She looked like a lost child—a vulnerable one at that, but he'd yet to find anyone prettier, or more appealing.

Did he want her for something?

A loaded question and one Trey would never answer.

"I was heading to town to buy feed for the horses, when I realized I hadn't given you the key to the house. But first," Trey said, placing his hands on her shoulders and turning her around so that her back was to him. He lifted her hair and slipped the necklace around her neck, letting the loose chain slide down her throat to fall into the soft valley between her breasts. He breathed in, a sharp intake of oxygen. Damn. His mind drifted to thoughts of putting his hands where the necklace lay and touching her soft skin there. Hell, he wanted to do more than merely touch her.

Wow . . . where had that come from? If only Trey wasn't a hard nose when it came to good, decent women. Maddie wasn't for him. So he removed all thoughts of lust out of his head. He wasn't about to let the subtle scent of Maddie's skin—a trace of sweet raspberries—and her vulnerable state affect him. He wouldn't do that to Maddie Brooks. She'd been through enough. "There," he said and stepped away.

Maddie turned around, removing her gloves so she could finger the charm. Joy lit her eyes, but she guarded her delight carefully, as if she were afraid to indulge in happiness for too long. Trey understood that better than she might guess.

"Thank you," she said with a small smile.

He nodded, keeping his eyes focused on her face and not on the deep inviting cleavage that framed the necklace. He slipped a hand into his pocket, coming up with a key ring. He removed one and handed it to her. "Here you go. Come and go as you please on the ranch. I won't wait up."

"Oh, I won't be going out much, unless I have to make a late-night house call."

He nodded again, not happy with the notion of Maddie Brooks underfoot every night. "Sometimes, I get in late," he admitted, "but if you need anything when I'm not around, you know Kit, my foreman?"

"Yes, we've met. But I'm sure I'll be fine."

"Okay then. I'd better get that grain before the store closes."

She lifted the key to the ranch house. "Thanks again. I guess I'll get my things from the Cactus Inn now."

Trey reached into his back pocket and presented her with his red bandanna. "For your face."

"Oh." Color rose from under her smudge marks, brightening her face to a rosy hue. "Is it that bad?"

"Doesn't bother me a bit. But I figured you'd want to clean up before heading to the motel."

She began swiping her face for all she was worth. "Thanks. I must look like heck."

Trey turned his back on Maddie, released a reluctant sigh and headed for his truck, mumbling, "*Heck* never looked so danged cute."

Trey got into his truck, gunned the engine and took off, his wheels spitting up a cloud of dry Texas dust. He'd come into town to help Maddie move her things from the motel. It hadn't set right that she'd refused his offer. What kind of man would allow a woman, who was down on her luck, alone in the world and who had lost most of her possessions, face that task alone?

But one look at her today, standing there in the midst of her onetime home and something powerful stabbed at him. It wasn't like anything he'd felt before, this protective, warm feeling he had for her. Trey didn't like it, not one bit. If he wasn't careful, he'd be under her spell, she'd be under his sheets, and then disaster would strike.

Maddie would come out the loser.

He didn't want to add to her troubles. As much as he wanted to help her, going to the motel wouldn't have been wise. Trey shook his head. Spending time with Maddie Brooks would just be dang foolish. He'd have to nip this problem in the bud, before anything dared to blossom.

Tonight, he'd lay things out straight with Maddie.

But in truth, he'd be more comfortable wrestling half a dozen big, hungry grizzly bears.

MADDIE WAS FINALLY going to see the inside of Trey's house at 2 Hope. She stepped through tall column pillars into a dwelling, beaten down from time and perhaps a bit of neglect.

Yet, undisguised warmth seemed to invite her in. Her heart squeezed tight as she stood in the entry, gazing at a massive stone fireplace, complete with a heavy beamed mantel and a wide accommodating hearth. The only thing missing from this picture was the moose head above the fireplace. Instinct told her Trey wouldn't approve or indulge in the hunting of innocent animals, thank goodness.

A slightly worn, completely comfortable-looking leather sofa graced the wall facing the fireplace, and antique pieces from days gone by surrounded the room. Maddie couldn't help feel like an invader, intruding on Trey's privacy, the total masculine feel of the room alluding to Trey's lone-wolf demeanor. A woman had no place here. There were no lace curtains or hand-sewn pillows, nothing feminine at all, yet the house had a welcoming, solid, lived-in feel. A house made for a man.

Maddie was certain Trey didn't want her living here.

But she had no other option. She had responsibilities, clients who depended on her to keep their animals healthy. There was no one else in Hope Wells to look after the animals of the twenty-odd ranches in the county. And just the other day, she'd had to neuter Randolph Curry's rambunctious Irish setter, before the neighbors shot the dang dog for lewd acts of conduct on the main streets in town. Then there was young Bessie Mallery's cat Lucky, who'd surprised everyone with a litter of seven. Maddie had had to untangle that feline's umbilical cord before it strangled three of the kittens. Fortunately Lucky's name had held true, and she hadn't lost any of her offspring, much to everyone's relief.

With a nod, Maddie concluded if she were to keep her practice going, she would have to accept Trey's hospitality. But she'd made a solemn vow to stick to her business and stay out of his way, until the time came when she could rebuild her own office in town.

"All set," Trey said, coming to stand before her. "I put everything inside your room. Down the hall, third door on the left."

"Thank you," Maddie offered. When she'd pulled up

just minutes ago with her oddball assortment of clothes, medical books, some veterinary equipment—the smaller tools of her trade she'd been able to salvage—Trey had been waiting on his front porch. He wouldn't allow her to lift a thing from the bed of her truck. He'd just reached in and grabbed everything, loading up his arms and telling her to make herself comfortable inside the house. "The house is nice, looks like it's been lived in some. I'll bet there's a batch of stories hidden in these old walls."

Maddie bit her lip and glanced away. She'd never been one to babble, but then she'd never felt this darn awkward before.

Trey grinned. "This house goes way back. It was one of the first ones built in Hope Wells back in the day when there was free range. I know a few stories, but they aren't fit for telling in polite company."

Maddie sighed, wondering what wonderfully sinful things had happened at 2 Hope years ago. "I'd love to hear them sometime."

Trey looked her over, and began shaking his head. With a dubious expression plastered on his face, he flat out refused. "No way, Maddie. You don't want to hear any of *those* stories."

Maddie fumed silently. She'd never shed her wholesome, good-girl image. The one time she'd tried transforming into a sexy siren, she'd failed miserably. Trey hadn't paid her any notice at all. She was over it, and him, but she wished that he would treat her the way he treated other women. She wasn't a child who needed protecting from vile stories. She wasn't a frail dove that needed rescuing. She was a strong woman who knew when to give up on a hopeless cause. Maddie had given up on Trey Walker.

"I think I'll put my things away now. Thanks, again." She moved past him, heading down the hallway.

"Dinner's at eight."

She swirled around. "Oh, I don't expect you to feed me."

"You have to eat."

"I . . . I guess I didn't think—"

"Kit and the guys are off tonight, so you're stuck with my cooking. With any luck, I'll manage not to poison the both of us."

An encouraging thought. "What's for dinner?"

"Stew?"

"I'll help and don't even dream of refusing the offer. It's the least I can do. After all, you're putting me up and allowing me to keep my practice running on your property. I certainly don't expect to be waited on. I want to pull my weight around here. Besides, I don't have a kitchen anymore, and I sort of miss cooking."

Hands on hips, Trey stared at her. "Are you through?"

Maddie's mouth dropped open. "Uh, yeah."

"Meet me in the kitchen in an hour."

She gulped then nodded. She couldn't tell if Trey was amused or annoyed at her little outburst. She had to remind herself that he was a man who wasn't accustomed to having a woman around, and he was probably already sorry he'd agreed to their deal.

"THIS IS HARDLY poison, Trey."

Trey riveted his eyes on Maddie polishing off her second bowl of son-of-a-gun stew. "And I never figured you for a liar."

He arched a brow. "Liar?"

"You can cook. I mean *really* cook. You had the meat marinating in this yummy sauce and then you did this amazing thing with the spices. I've never had better stew."

"You helped," Trey said, standing to take his plate to the sink.

Maddie immediately rose and gently grabbed the plate from his hand. "All I did was cut up potatoes and carrots. Essentially, you made the meal, so I'm going to do all of the cleanup. It's the least—"

"I know, it's the least you can do."

"Yes, so please sit down, and I'll pour your coffee. It'll take me only a minute to have this kitchen back in order."

Maddie brought him a mug of steaming hot coffee—cream, no sugar, just the way he liked it. Trey decided to sit, rather than argue. He sipped from his coffee and watched her bustle about his kitchen. Wasn't too often a woman graced his kitchen. In fact, the last time he could recall was when his father had married wife number four, and they'd held the wedding here at the ranch. Then, there'd been a wagonload of women in the kitchen, caterers and servers alike, cooking up the wedding feast.

The marriage had lasted all of ten months. Hell, Trey couldn't even remember the gal's name exactly. Elisa, Elena, something with an E.

"How's the coffee?" Maddie asked as she bent down to load the dishwasher.

Trey's gaze fastened on the derriere pointing in his direction. He couldn't quite help watching the wiggle as she shifted to make room for more plates. He had a tantalizing view of her backside, and petite as Maddie was, everything she had was perfectly proportioned. Her tank top pulled up as she bent and a slice of skin appeared in the gap at the small of her back. The combination of her wiggling behind and that particular delicate area, newly exposed, caused Trey a moment of grief and that grief was growing harder by the second.

"Coffee's fine," he managed.

She closed the dishwasher door and lifted up. *Thank you.* Trey gulped down the rest of his coffee, landing his mug down on the table with a thud.

Maddie appeared before him with the coffeepot in hand. "Another cup?"

Before he could answer, she leaned over to begin pouring. That damn silver horse she wore around her neck caught his eye as it swung out. He followed the glint until the charm settled right smack in the deep hollow between her breasts.

His grief intensified.

He wasn't used to having a pretty woman around, helping with the meals, serving him in his kitchen as though she really belonged here. This cozy domestic scene would give him hives if he wasn't careful. And the last thing he needed was to walk around stiff between the legs all day.

He reached out and took hold of Maddie's wrist. "Sit down, Maddie. We need to talk."

Maddie's eyes grew wide, probably from the sharpness of his tone. She sat in a chair across from him and suddenly Trey felt older than his thirty-one years. He opened his mouth to begin, but a commotion coming from the corral had him clamping his mouth down. He listened as his stallion whinnied and snorted, kicking up a fuss. Trey bounded up from his seat.

"Storm's fixing to have a tirade. I'd better go check on him."

Trey headed to the corral quickly, knowing what damage his feisty stallion could do. He reached the fence just as Storm lifted his front legs up in a flurry, snorting loudly, disturbing the quiet of the night.

"Hey, boy. Simmer down," he cooed, trying to soothe the stallion's ire.

Storm took note of him, pranced around the perimeter

of the corral then stomped, sifting dirt with his front hooves, communicating to Trey the only way he knew how. "I know how you feel, boy. But I can't let you out. Not with the way you're all tangled up inside."

Trey whistled softly, an old cowboy tune he'd learned as a child, the melody something Storm recognized. The horse snorted again and pranced against the wind, his ink-black mane catching the moonlight.

He was a thing of beauty, Storm. His restless nature proved him wild at heart, an animal that didn't hold much trust. Trey understood that horse better than he did most people.

"He's a free spirit." The gentle voice came from behind.

Trey turned, noting Maddie standing in the shadows. She stepped closer, carefully, with one eye on Storm. Trey trusted her not to spook the horse. Leaning against the fence, he rested his arms on the top rail. "We understand each other."

Maddie smiled. "I guess I know what you mean."

Trey nodded. "I guess you do."

Storm had pretty much settled down, his tirade all but over. He pranced a bit more, showing off his beautiful grace and agility probably for Maddie's sake. He didn't blame the horse for trying to impress the lady.

"Do you ride him?" Maddie ventured closer, taking up space next to him by the fence.

Trey chuckled. "He doesn't care much for riders."

"Have you had him long?"

"Less than a month. I went to a cattle auction, took one look at the stallion and that was that. I had to have him. His previous owner said he'll never be *all* yours. It was what I liked best about him."

What he didn't add was Storm's owner had practically given the horse to Trey, having had his fill of the wild, unruly stallion.

Maddie smiled then called softly to the horse. "Hey, Storm. Here, boy."

She put out her hand, reaching beyond the fence.

Much to Trey's amazement, Storm wandered over, coming to stand before her. "Careful, he doesn't know you."

Maddie placed her boots on the lower rung of the fence rail and lifted up, coming eye to eye with the stallion. She reached out gingerly, smart enough not to touch the feisty animal, and the horse snorted, as if taking in her scent, each one completely aware of the other. "There, boy. You just need some attention, don't you? All alone out here in this corral."

Maddie's voice, her calm demeanor, her confidence with the now sedate animal, impressed the hell out of Trey. He'd seen her work with animals before and it never ceased to amaze him. She had special qualities.

Trey swallowed hard, watching her speak softly, her delicate hands reaching out in a nonthreatening way, until Storm allowed her a touch. She slid her hands slowly, carefully, without hesitation over Storm's mane. The stallion snorted, stomped, but didn't back off. He allowed her a brief stroke, one time, before racing off.

Maddie smiled warmly, her heart-shaped mouth turning up with genuine affection. "He knows me now. I think I've made a new friend."

Trey's groin tightened. His mouth went bone-dry. Maddie cuddling with his wild stallion was a sight to behold. The last thing he wanted was to have lusty thoughts about Maddie Brooks. She had a gentle nature, one he couldn't destroy. "About that talk . . . ."

Maddie's smile evaporated as she glanced one last time at Storm. She jumped down from the fence, but the heel of her boot caught on the fence rung just as a gust of wind blew by and she lost her balance. Trey caught her just before she tumbled, his hand brushing the swell of her breast. He wrapped her tight against him, relishing her small, delicate body against his big frame. "Whoa. The wind nearly blew you over. You okay?"

Trey forced himself to release her and step back. She stared up at him, her eyes gleaming, her face lifting up to his and that perfect mouth trembling slightly. "I'm . . . okay. You wanted to have a talk?"

Yeah, he needed to talk to her. He needed to lay things on the line, leaving no room for doubt that this was strictly a business arrangement. He needed to protect her from the Walker Curse. In the long run, she'd be better off. And so would he. Maddie wasn't a woman to fool with. But the words that had played out in his mind a dozen times wouldn't come. They stuck in his throat like a mouthful of dry cotton. He opened his mouth then clamped down.

His fingers still tingled from where he'd touched the soft small slope of her breasts and his body shook with powerful need. He couldn't tear his gaze away from that lovely, upturned face. He simply stared, swallowing hard, a colossal debate warring in his head. He didn't get it—this unwelcome need he had for her. Maddie in the moonlight was a beautiful thing, but it was something else, something more powerful that drew him to her. He wanted to hold her again. To feel her softness crushed against him. The need inside him was great and all of his hard won mental rules slipped away instantly.

Maddie Brooks was the last woman on Earth he should touch.

But he wanted her. Just once.

He leaned in, bending to cup the back of her head with his hand. Her silky hair fell against his palm as he gently tilted her up, toward him.

"'Trey, what are you doing?" she asked, her voice a breathless whisper against his lips.

"Being a damn fool."

Then he brushed his mouth over hers.

Chapter Two

TREY PULLED HER up against him and brought his lips down, taking her in a dreamy kiss that belied every single fantasy she'd ever had about the elusive cowboy. Their bodies brushed intimately as Trey made his claim. Confusing and wonderful, mystifying and breathtaking thoughts rushed into Maddie's head.

She fell into his kiss like a thirsty woman given a tall, cool drink and imbibed heartily, kissing him back, pressing her lips against his with equal passion and desire. She'd dreamed of this too many times to count. Feeling his heat, the gentle way he commanded and possessed her, went beyond anything Maddie might have imagined. In her heart of hearts, she'd always known Trey Walker could turn her inside out.

If he was a damn fool as he'd claimed, then Maddie was easily out of her mind. Trey toyed with Maddie's long hair, stroking the strands and then taking a fistful. The playful tug then release triggered rippling waves of electricity throughout her body and a soft moan tumbled from her lips.

Trey wedged his body closer, tightening the gap, meshing fully against her as he continued to kiss her. He coaxed her lips open, and when their tongues mated she braced herself against the onslaught of his passion, the erotic joining being almost too much to bear. A completely male sound escaped his throat and Maddie too was lost.

Moonlight beamed down in soft rays, and in the background, Maddie heard Storm whinny and stomp his front legs before taking off in a fast run around the corral. The stallion had a spirit all its own. Wild and untamed and one with the land, so much like Trey Walker.

Maddie lifted her arms up grazing Trey's shoulder, her fingers dipping into dark wavy locks of hair at the base of his neck. He smiled into her mouth, obviously pleased with her display, and slanted his mouth once again over hers, taking her in another long, deep, sexy kiss.

Maddie breathed in his scent, leather and earth—so raw, so masculine, so completely Trey. He was a man's man, a special breed who knew how to please a woman. As his lips claimed hers once more, Maddie realized that she could easily fall under his spell again.

Too soon, Trey pulled away and cool Texas air replaced his body's heat. They stood there, facing each other, eyes locked, hearts beating.

Trey blinked.

Maddie tried for a smile, but his expression wouldn't allow it. He appeared shaken, taken completely unaware. So many expressions crossed his features that Maddie didn't know what to think. She didn't know what to say, either. Moments ticked by and then Trey finally broke the silence. He stood with his head bent, scratching his neck in the same spot where Maddie's fingers had explored just seconds ago. "That was entirely my fault. A big mistake."

Maddie crossed her arms over her middle and stood her ground. She may not have had an abundance of experience with men but she had excellent female intuition, and Trey Walker wasn't getting away with this. He *wanted* her. And he wasn't so much of a fool not to see that she *wanted* him back. Finally, after all this time, Trey had come around. She didn't know why exactly, because for the past year he hadn't given her the time of day but suddenly Trey had taken notice.

What they shared tonight was something short of heaven. Maddie hadn't felt anything like this before. And she wasn't about to allow Trey to deny it. "It didn't *feel* like a mistake."

Trey's head snapped up. "Well, it was."

"Are you saying you didn't want to kiss me?"

"No. I mean . . . yes. What I'm saying is that it shouldn't have happened."

"But it did, Trey. It happened."

He sighed. "Maddie."

Maddie took one step forward, keeping her eyes on his face. She spoke softly. "I liked it, in case you didn't notice."

He swallowed, his gaze locking onto her lips. "I noticed."

Trey Walker had turned her life upside down this past year. She needed to know how he felt inside. She needed to hear the words. She smiled and spoke softly again, taking a brief glance below his belt buckle. "And I noticed how much *you* liked it."

Trey's brows shot up. She might have shocked him.

"Okay, damn it. It was hot. Probably the hottest kiss I've ever . . . it doesn't matter, Maddie. We're business partners and I shouldn't have taken such liberties. That's what I wanted to talk to you about before Storm acted up."

Her nerves twitching, Maddie's voice rose. "*That* was what you wanted to talk about. You and me, kissing?"

What was Trey trying to do, add insult to injury? He'd just kissed her senseless, probably ruining her for any other man, and now after giving her a small taste of heaven, he wanted to tuck her safely away and pretend nothing had happened. He wanted to make sure that nothing like it would ever happen again.

"Not exactly. I wanted us to sit down and have a logical, *reasonable* discussion about our living arrangements. I've never had a woman live out here with me and well, I suppose it's a fact of nature that in a weak moment . . . " He paused, taking a breath of air, before continuing. "What I mean to say is that the only way this is going to work is if we keep our distance. I wanted to make sure you saw it the same way."

With chin held high, Maddie stepped closer until she stood boot to boot with him. "You call kissing a girl until her knees buckle keeping your distance?"

Trey focused on her mouth. "I'm taking all the blame." And those incredible intense eyes softened. "It was a great kiss, Maddie. But wrong."

"If you knew it was wrong then why'd you do it?"

Trey looked away. And they were immersed in silence. Only Storm's occasional quiet snort could be heard. Patiently, Maddie waited.

Trey turned and his dark eyes pierced hers. This time she knew she'd have the truth. "I've wanted to kiss you for a long time."

Maddie's heart lurched. She hadn't expected to hear him admit anything of the sort. All of this time, he'd been aloof and detached, giving her no reason to hope. He'd spoken about having a weak moment, but now Maddie knew it wasn't just that. He'd been thinking about her, just as she'd been thinking about him. "You have?"

He nodded and spoke with firm conviction. "But it isn't right."

"Why, Trey? Why isn't it right?" she asked, trying to puzzle through Trey's admission.

Trey shook his head, his expression filled with regret. He softened his tone, but his words cut straight through her heart. "Because wanting you and doing right by you are two different things. It's best you understand that. I'm not the man for you, Maddie. I never could be."

Trey stalked off and headed to the older barn, leaving Maddie standing there in the moonlight. He'd made a world-class mess out of things and he'd hurt Maddie in the process. Nothing about this night had turned out as he'd hoped. Why couldn't he have left well enough alone? Why'd he have to kiss her? His body still hummed from the impact of that kiss, the soft sweet way Maddie had given herself to him. The way she told him with every movement, every little moan, that it could only get better.

That kiss blew his mind.

Trey's well-honed control had been tested to the limit and had failed. Miserably. One petite little redhead had thrown him off-kilter. She'd made him hard. She'd made him want.

It had been a long time since Trey had taken up with a woman. He'd made a pact long ago that "temporary" involvement was all he could manage. One-night stands were even better. Not that he'd indulged lately, but he knew that sticking to his plan, especially with Maddie, would benefit everyone and hurt no one. Trey's vow to keep his distance couldn't be sharper or laid out more clearly because now he understood what kissing her was like.

Trey walked to the stall that housed one of Maddie's patients. "Hey there, Maggie. How're you doing, girl?"

The fair-haired dog looked up with big, sad eyes. She'd

been accidentally shot with a round of birdshot by Willy McGill, a young boy who'd been playing with his daddy's gun.

"Feeling any better tonight?"

Trey bent to scratch the old girl behind the ears, gently stroking her coat. "The doc fixed you up real good. You'll be going home soon."

Trey stood and checked on all of the other animals, making note of how well cared for they all appeared. After the fire that had claimed Maddie's office, Trey had worked like a demon to get this place ready for the animals, mucking out the stalls, cleaning them the best he could. He'd laid down blankets for the larger animals and gathered up cages that he had on the grounds for the smaller ones. Of the eight stalls, more than half were filled with animals on the mend.

The tack room in the back served double-duty as Maddie's office and an examining room. She'd brought in what few supplies she'd salvaged, others she'd purchased including a makeshift examining table made of heavy aluminum. She had all that she needed to start up her practice again.

Trey shouldn't lose sight of that. He shouldn't forget the good Maddie coming to 2 Hope Ranch would serve. The animals needed her expert care. The deal he and Maddie had made insured the animals would receive it.

In the year since Doc Benning had left Hope Wells, Maddie's practice had grown. She'd gained a reputation as a compassionate, intelligent veterinarian who loved all animals and had special talents communicating with them. She'd been young, coming straight out of college, but it hadn't taken her long to earn the town's trust. And for the time being, she'd be working here, treating the animals.

And living with him.

Trey would just learn to adjust.

MADDIE ENTERED THE kitchen through the back door and glanced at the coffee cups that had been left on the table. All of this had started by Storm's sudden outburst. The stallion had interrupted what would have been Trey's attempt at setting up their "business" arrangement. What he'd really wanted to do was lay down the rules. "Rules" that, according to Trey Walker, were not to be compromised or challenged. "Rules" that left no doubt in Maddie's mind that the cowboy simply was not interested.

She cleared the coffee cups and loaded them in the dishwasher. Then she refilled the sugar bowl and creamer and put them away, straightening up the kitchen the best she could, keeping her vow to pitch in and share in fifty percent of the daily chores. She owed Trey that much. He'd been kind and generous coming to her aid when she'd needed help the most.

Her mind still raced at one hundred miles per hour.

She doubted she'd be able to concentrate on one single

thing tonight, other than Trey's incredible kiss. Maddie would never forget that earth-moving, heart-stopping experience, but it seemed that for Trey, it hadn't been enough. It hadn't been what he wanted. Maddie would have to respect his wishes. She was here at 2 Hope living off his hospitality, with a roof over her head and, more importantly, a place to treat the animals.

That mattered to her above all else.

With the kitchen clean, Maddie headed for her bedroom, taking one last peek out the window. Storm pranced and snorted, making his way around the perimeter of the corral, his shiny, sleek mane catching starlight.

"He'll never be *all* yours," Trey had been told.

How well Maddie understood that. The stallion's instinct, his spirit, the very heart of the animal, wouldn't allow it. Stallions could be trained, but they could never be fully trusted. Just when you believed them tame, their wild side would emerge, creating havoc and fear. An untamed spirit exposed their true temperament—one that thrived solely on strength, independence, and freedom. Storm belonged to no one but himself.

And Maddie realized now what Trey had seen in Storm. He'd seen himself.

MADDIE WOKE EARLY the next morning after a restless night.

She'd never been one for change, and sleeping in a strange bed in someone else's home hadn't been as easy as she'd hoped. She missed her small apartment in town. She missed her things. Almost everything she loved had gone up in smoke. She'd never again see her favorite rhinestone hairclip that had kept her bangs out of her eyes on her first date ever, with Johnny Renato. She'd never slip her feet into her worked-in jogging shoes that had accompanied her on miles and miles of asphalt road. She'd never put her arms through her cozy chenille bathrobe and snuggle herself tight on a cold, lonely night. She missed her books too, especially the mysteries that kept her from sleep and the romance novels that made her dreams so sweet. And how odd was it that she missed her dry college textbooks?

She brought her fingers up to the silver charm resting against her chest. Aphrodite hugged her neck holding tender memories of her grandmother close. Gratitude that the necklace had been spared in the fire bubbled up inside of her. It was sort of a miracle.

As she glanced around the spacious bedroom that would now be her home, that gratitude continued. A good-size bed with a thick, hand-quilted paisley comforter kept her warm throughout the night. Her meager belongings were housed in a lovely carved-oak armoire that stood against the opposing wall. The armoire's intricate workmanship spoke of decades past, giving the room a sense of history.

Maddie's gaze drifted to a vase atop the armoire filled

with a bouquet of fresh pastel carnations. Trey had put them there sometime yesterday as a gesture of welcome and they actually helped her feel a little less like an imposition to him.

In so many ways, Trey Walker was a mystery to her—an unreadable man that rarely let his guard down and rarely allowed anyone inside. He'd given her a taste of it last night by pulling her into a deep passionate kiss, then closing up tight and not giving her a glimpse of his true feelings. He'd pushed her away and, okay, she'd definitely gotten the message. She'd try to forget the wonderful kiss and his strong embrace, though she didn't think it'd be easy. If a cordial businesslike relationship was all he wanted, she would have to respect that.

Sunlight beamed in bright and warm through the shuttered window. The morning would slide by if she wasn't careful. Today was her first official day on the job since the fire. So why was she lollygagging? "Maddie, get a move on. You have things to do," she uttered.

Maddie tossed off the covers, rose from the bed and grinned like a fool, suddenly eager to start her day. She hugged her chest against the cool morning air and strode down the hallway in her bare feet and pajamas.

Thoughts of a steamy shower filled her mind as she opened the bathroom door and strode inside. She stopped mid-stride, a gasp tearing from her throat. "Oh! Sorry."

Trey stood facing the mirror with razor in hand, the unshaven half of his face still lathered up with white foam.

Fresh lime permeated the air, the soapy clean scent appealing to all of her female senses. Trey glanced her way for one second then faced the mirror again, taking a swipe at his beard and examining his progress.

"Nothing to be sorry for, Maddie. I should've been up and out early this morning. Would have been if the pipe hadn't busted in the other bathroom. Now it looks like we'll be sharing this one until I get the plumbing fixed."

"Oh, that's alright," Maddie said numbly. When she'd made this bargain with Trey he'd offered her this bathroom, closest to the bedrooms during her stay, while he had opted to use the one nearest the kitchen. "I hope it isn't too serious."

But as she looked at him, Maddie knew it was *serious*. Tearing her gaze away from the wide expanse of Trey's solid chest was proving seriously impossible. Tiny hairs curled around his nipples and arrowed down his torso, leading below his waist and into a tight pair of unbuttoned jeans. Tall, tanned, muscular Trey was seriously taking her breath away.

"Don't know. My uncle Monty's the expert. He can fix just about anything." Trey took another swipe at his beard then rinsed the razor in the sink. "I gave him a call, but he can't get out here until next week." He stopped shaving to turn to her. "If it's a problem, I'll call in a plumber today."

"Not a problem at all." She actually sounded unaffected seeing his half-naked, sexy body. After all, he'd set down the rules last night and she wasn't going to complicate his life by swooning over him, even if it killed her. She shrugged. "I'll shower later."

The last thing she wanted was to be a burden. Or cost Trey any money. She knew from their deal that Trey wasn't in good financial shape right now and hiring a plumber could get expensive. If need be, she'd share the bathroom but she'd make darn sure not to barge in on him again.

Maddie turned to leave, but Trey stopped her. "Maddie?"

She looked up. "Yes?"

Trey leaned both hands on the tiled counter and bent his head, staring into the sink. Half-shaven, bare-chested and more tempting than Maddie wanted to admit, he spoke softly, "About last night—"

With a tilt of her head, Maddie finished his thought. "It was a mistake."

His head snapped up and he studied her for a moment. "Right."

"And it'll never happen again."

He hesitated. "Right."

"Anything else?" She asked on tiptoes, ready to turn and make a quick retreat.

Trey glanced at her lips then let out a breath. "Just that I think it's best that we move forward and forget about—"

"Already done, Trey. It's forgotten."

"That easy?"

The question seemed to have slipped from his tongue and if he could have pulled the words back, Maddie was certain he would have.

She lifted her lips in a quick smile. "Easy as peach pie," she said and headed back to her bedroom.

She heard the shower door open then close, the sound of water raining down. Maddie couldn't block out the image of one naked cowboy soaping up in a hot, steamy shower. Her heart pounded hard against her chest as she shut her bedroom door then leaned heavily against it and closed her eyes. "Easy as peach pie," she repeated on a whisper. "Maddie Brooks, you are such a terrible liar."

Chapter Three

"It's Dr. Maddie! Mommy, Dr. Maddie is here!"

Annabelle Portman raced straight into Maddie's legs as she stepped down from her truck. The four-year-old clung on and hugged tight.

Maddie patted Annabelle's head. "Hey there, sweetie. How's my favorite helper?"

Annabelle beamed. "I groomed-ed Dumpling, and Mommy said I did a good job." And then the child's expression fell. "But now her leg is broke. Mommy said you can fix her."

Maddie bent down to the child's level, looking her straight in the eyes. "I'm going to do the best I can, Annabelle. Dumpling's a healthy horse and she probably just pulled up lame."

"That's what I think, Maddie. At least it's what I'm hoping," Caroline Portman said as she approached the truck. Maddie straightened and smiled at her good friend. She and Caroline had met on the first day Maddie arrived in Hope Wells. They'd nearly collided on the main street in town, their cars missing each other by mere inches and both women had instantly realized how lucky they'd been, not winding up in a hospital that day. They'd gone to lunch after that and had been close friends ever since.

"Hi," Maddie said, wrapping her arms around Caroline in a warm embrace. "It's good to see you."

And Maddie meant it with her whole heart. There weren't too many constants in Maddie's life right now, with the fire, losing nearly everything she owned, then coming to live with Trey, a man who would surely cause her more than one sleepless night. A visit with a good friend was just what Maddie needed today.

"It's great to see you, too. I've been planning on having you out for dinner, but dear sweet Dumpling beat me to it. She's in the barn and I've got her iced, using one of my old pant legs sewn up, just like you said. The ice pack seems to be working fine."

Annabelle giggled. "Dumpling looks funny wearing Mommy's pants."

"I bet she does," Maddie agreed with a grin, "but it's the best way to make her leg feel better."

"I'm hoping it's a sprain. It seemed warm to the touch," Caroline responded.

"Did she flinch when you applied pressure?" Maddie asked.

Caroline nodded. "And she gave me a sour look to boot."

Maddie reached for Annabelle's hand. "Well then, let's go take a look."

As they headed for the barn, Caroline said, "I wasn't sure you'd be ready for business yet. How are things at 2 Hope?"

"I set up my office this morning." She explained with a wry smile, "Of course, that took all of ten minutes, since I'm pretty much starting from scratch. There isn't too much going into my file cabinet just yet. But I've got a barn full of animals that need my attention."

With a tilt of her head, Caroline asked, "And are they the only ones getting your attention?"

Maddie knew what her friend hinted at. She'd shared with Caroline a little of her previous fascination with Trey. She couldn't blame Caroline for her curiosity and she wondered if small-town tongues were wagging over the situation. After all, she'd moved in with Trey Walker, the most eligible bachelor in three counties. "I hate to disappoint, but there's not much happening there."

"Hmmm. We'll have lunch after you take a look at Dumpling and you can tell me all about it."

An hour later, Maddie sat in the Portman kitchen relieved that Dumpling hadn't broken any bones. "Dumpling should be fine in a few days. Just use the heating liniment I gave you. Massage it in really good and it'll improve her circulation."

"I'm glad it wasn't more serious," Caroline said, setting two plates of fried chicken salad down on the table. "And thanks for including Annabelle. Letting her help out makes her feel kind of special. And Lord knows that child needs to feel special, after her father up and left us both last year."

"Yeah, that's got to be hard on her. Do you ever hear from Gil?"

Caroline glanced out the kitchen window, watching her daughter skip rope. She twisted her mouth and lowered her voice. "He calls to speak with Annabelle every month or so but he hasn't seen her since he left. Guess I wasn't such a good judge of character, was I?"

"It wasn't your fault, Caroline."

Caroline set the napkins and utensils down along with two glasses of iced tea then took a seat to face Maddie. "I think it was. He wasn't ready to settle down. And maybe I pushed him a little too hard."

"He's a grown man, responsible for his own actions. You can't deny that. A real man should know what's in his own heart. He shouldn't play games."

She laughed and cast Maddie a direct look. "Are we still speaking about Gil?"

Maddie blushed. "Maybe." She smiled as she sipped her tea. "Maybe not."

Caroline leaned in, bracing her elbows on the table. "You know I'm dying of curiosity. What's it like living with Trey?"

"I've only been there one night."

"Sometimes, that's all it takes," her friend said with a twinkle in her blue eyes.

Maddie gulped down. At times, it seemed Caroline could read her mind. Or maybe she was capable of reading Maddie's guilty expression. She really wasn't good at hiding things. "Okay, something happened last night, but it's not worth talking about."

"Let me decide what's not worth talking about. I'm knee-deep in Talking Elmo and Candyland. I love my daughter dearly, but a girl's got to have an adult conversation once in a while. So, what happened?"

"He kissed me," Maddie confessed.

Caroline's blonde brows drew up. "Already? I thought that might take a week or two."

"*A week or two*? Are you serious? It was the last thing in the world I ever expected from Trey Walker. It really threw me. He admitted that he'd wanted to kiss me for a long time, but after he did, well, he backed way off. He says it was a big mistake and that we need to keep things strictly business."

"Really? Doesn't sound that way to me. Unless . . . the kiss wasn't any good."

Heat crawled up Maddie's neck. She'd been thinking about that kiss all morning. "Oh, it was good."

"How good?"

"Better than cool summer rain. Better than hot chocolate by the fire. Better than . . . anything," Maddie admitted on a whisper. Then she straightened in her seat and said with certainty, "But it's over and done with. We've come to an understanding."

"For as long as that lasts. I've known Trey a long time, Maddie, and if he kissed you, he's interested. That man isn't into playing games. He's about as serious as they come. He doesn't let women get too close, but then, he's probably never met anyone quite like you before."

"Yeah, the wholesome girl-next-door."

"Correction, the girl-in-the-next-bedroom. Be careful, honey. You're probably scaring the stuffing out of him. I wouldn't want to see you with a broken heart."

"That's exactly what I'm doing. I'm being very careful."

AN ORANGE GOLD burst of color set low on the horizon as Maddie pulled up to the barn at 2 Hope and parked her truck. Hopping down, she slammed the door shut, a pleasing tune strumming through her head. She'd had a successful day making house calls to neighboring ranches, checking on her more recent cases and making sure everyone knew how to reach her in the event of an emergency. She'd given out her cell phone number, making certain to always have her phone on hand now.

She should be hearing soon about the insurance claim she filed and hopefully the money would come through for her to rebuild her office in town. With that thought in mind, she headed toward the barn door, anxious to check on Maggie and the other animals one last time before she closed up for the night.

As she rounded the corner of the barn, she bumped into

Trey's granite chest. The thump sent her spiraling back and reaching for balance. She couldn't hold on. She went down, sprawling with a thud. A mound of straw cushioned her head against solid, packed dirt underneath.

Stung by embarrassment, Maddie tried to lift up, hoping to make a quick getaway, but Trey was immediately by her side, gently pressing her head back down. "Don't try to get up," he said with quiet authority, bending on one knee. "Lie still a minute and let me see if you've got a bump."

With nimble fingers, Trey worked his way through her hair, searching her head. She closed her eyes mortified at this awkward position and fascinated by the tender way he moved his hands through her strands. "I'm sorry, Maddie. I didn't see you coming."

She opened her eyes and stared at him. She saw so much in those deep dark eyes—emotions that he held back, concern that he'd tried to hide as he continued to probe for injuries. "I thought I was the doctor here," she said, cocking her mouth up slightly.

Trey sighed, shaking his head.

"I'm fine, Trey. Really. My mama used to say I'd be two days early for my own wedding, 'cause I'm always on the go, always rushing around. I've got to learn to slow down."

"And I've got to pay more attention."

Trey paid attention then, perusing her body, his gaze traveling slowly over her, lingering in places that made Maddie's heart race. "Are you hurt anywhere?"

"Just my pride. You pack a wallop, Trey Walker."

Trey grinned then, a sudden quick beautiful smile that left Maddie wanting more. "So I've been told. But I usually don't knock over petite females. Especially, not when I've come to ask a favor."

Maddie lifted up then, but none too quickly. Trey had a hand on her shoulder, slowly guiding her up to a sitting position. "A favor?"

"Yep," he said, standing and then lending a hand to help her up. Maddie wasn't too prideful to accept his help. She still felt a little shaky, her head swimming from the fall. Trey held her firm, making sure she felt secure on both legs, before releasing her hand. "I found a young heifer on the south pasture tangled up in barbed wire. I released her the best I know how, but there's a deep wound. It'll wait. You're in no shape to work right now. I'll go back and check on her later."

"I'll be fine in a minute," Maddie said, as a wave of dizziness struck. Her legs nearly buckled then and Trey grabbed for her.

"Whoa," he said, holding her steady. Then in a quick move, Trey lifted her up into his arms.

"What are you doing?" she asked, hazy from the fall, but even more hazy from being in Trey's strong arms once again. That heady mix of leather and earth wafted down to her, the scent being Trey's alone. She felt safe and secure and silly all at the same time.

"Making sure you sit down and rest." He carried her to the front porch and planted her gently into a wicker love seat that had seen better days. A fleeting thought crossed Maddie's mind that the bench seat could use a woman's touch, some soft material and a bit of lace. She thought the same of Trey—he too could use a woman's touch. Although he held her with such care, such tenderness, he was a hard man who thrived on his solitude. She envied the woman who might eventually soften him.

To her surprise, Trey took the seat next to her. His long legs spread wide, he leaned back with his arm resting on the back of the love seat. A minute passed in silence before he faced her.

"I'm not used to having a woman around here, Maddie. It'll take some getting used to. I might've guessed you'd be around the barn, but I barreled around it like—"

"Like you owned the place," Maddie said with a smile.

Trey laughed, his dark eyes gleaming through fading sunlight. "Well, yeah."

"No need to apologize, Trey. It was an accident."

"How's the head now?" he asked, his gaze locked onto hers.

"Better," she said truthfully. "I'm not dizzy anymore."

"That's good." He leaned forward and studied her, his focus moving down to her mouth and lingering. Maddie's blood pumped hard, roaring in her ears. She held her breath anticipating his next move, hoping for another kiss. Trey bent closer and reached up, his hand going into her hair and a red-hot rush of heat warmed her belly.

Trey pulled a strand of straw from her head.

He stared at it. "Looks like I drew the short straw, Maddie."

"Does that mean you lose?"

Trey glanced at her mouth one last time. He nodded and stood to leave. "Yeah, it means I lose."

MADDIE BROOKS WAS the damnedest, most stubborn woman Trey had come across in years. Not one hour after he'd nearly squashed the tiny woman like a bug, she'd insisted on seeing to the wounded heifer. With him or without him, she'd threatened, she was heading for the south pasture.

With him, he'd decided without question. The sun had set and the road wasn't easy to navigate. They drove in his Chevy truck over rough terrain, Trey taking cursory glances at Maddie, making certain she was up to the bumpy drive. One thing he noticed about the redhead, she was determined and no amount of dissuading on his part would work. He worried each time she lifted a hand to her head, if even to brush hair from her face.

He recalled probing for bumps earlier, the soft silky strands of dark ginger flowing through his hands. The sensation had wrapped around him, and he found himself wanting again.

He'd wanted to kiss her. He'd wanted to lift her up into his arms and instead of depositing her in that love seat, he'd wanted to see how she looked out of her blue jeans and tiny T-shirt, lying on his bed. To see those soft silky strands of hair flow over his pillow.

But Trey had drawn the short straw when it came to women like Maddie Brooks. He'd saved them both by denying his impulse earlier and kissing her. Maddie would've come out the loser in the end, and Trey wasn't going to let that happen. The woman had already lost enough.

"Are we close?" she asked, her eyes probing through the darkness for signs of the injured animal.

He pulled to a stop and searched the area where the barbed-wire fence needed repair. "It's right here," he said. Then he climbed down from the truck and came around to the passenger door to help Maddie. She handed him her medical bag and then jumped down unaided.

Stubborn.

Trey lit a butane lamp and guided Maddie to where the heifer lay wounded on the ground.

"Hey there, little one," Maddie said softly as she bent to see the extent of the injury. Trey sat down cross-legged and placed the Hereford's head in his lap while Maddie opened her medical bag. "Looks like you have a deep gash here." She stroked the heifer's withers softly as seconds became minutes.

Under Maddie's patient loving touch, the frightened animal soon relaxed, and Trey sensed a bond of trust developing, as crazy as that might seem.

Maddie glanced at Trey. "Most of the time the cuts heal on their own, but this is a three-corner tear and needs clipping or it won't heal properly."

Trey watched as Maddie worked diligently, cutting away the flap of skin hanging as well as the surrounding hairs. She cleaned the area with a solution and applied an antiseptic with tender care. "There now," she said, finishing up. "We need to keep the wound clean and dry. The antiseptic is a fly repellent as well, but I'd feel better keeping an eye on her for at least a week. Do you think we can get her into the back of the truck?"

Trey nodded. "Let me get a blanket and lay it down in the bed."

Maddie stayed with the animal, soothing her with kind words and stroking her head while Trey prepared the bed of his truck. When he returned, he found the heifer standing upright, nudging her nose into Maddie's leg. He chuckled. "How did you do that?"

"Do what?" she replied with an innocent expression.

"I didn't think she'd be able to stand. I couldn't get her up when I found her out here earlier."

"Oh, she and I have come to an understanding," Maddie said with a smile. She moved toward the back of the truck and the wounded heifer followed. Maddie climbed up first and Trey had no trouble, heavy as the young heifer was, lifting her up and placing her inside the bed. She immediately walked to Maddie's side and lay down next to her on the blanket.

Trey shook his head and closed the tailgate shaking his head at Maddie's mastery.

He drove slowly back to the ranch, trying to avoid as many ditches and bumps as possible for Maddie's sake. He still hadn't gotten over knocking her down and almost out. Trey had never hurt a woman in his life. Not physically, anyway.

But he'd hurt one or two emotionally and he was dead set against allowing that to ever happen again. He'd been engaged once, and they'd almost married, which would have been a big mistake. But then Trey had been ten years younger, less experienced and a bit naive regarding the Walker Curse. He'd let everyone close convince him marriage was what he'd wanted. What had ensued afterward had been a disaster. He'd hurt his fiancé and nearly alienated everyone he cared about in the process.

Glancing through the back window of the cab, Trey took note of Maddie sitting with her head bent speaking to the heifer. "Damn amazing woman," he said.

Amazing with animals.

Amazing to look at.

Amazing to touch.

Lord only knew what other amazing things Maddie

could do.

And then his father's dying words rushed into his head in haunting fashion. "Don't make the same mistakes I made, son."

Trey was immediately reminded of his solemn vow to steer clear of her and keep their arrangement strictly business.

And no matter how amazing he found Maddie to be, Trey would honor that vow.

Chapter Four

MADDIE IMMERSED HERSELF in her work, having little time to do much else but fall into bed at night. She'd been on the ranch for five days now and things were finally settling into a routine. She and Trey had a polite, but distant relationship. She believed Trey admired her skills as a competent veterinarian, and she knew him to be an expert rancher. They had mutual respect for one another, but they made sure not to let things get too personal. Over their brief dinners at night, they'd speak about their work, his livestock and her cases, the weather, the newest reality television show. But they shied away from any private subjects.

Trey employed four ranch hands, all of whom lived off the ranch with their own families. On occasion, the foreman named Kit would stay to fix supper and chew the fat with his boss. Maddie had come to know Kit Carver from her visits to 2 Hope in the past and considered him more friend than acquaintance now.

But tonight Trey and his foreman had taken off after the evening meal. Maddie had offered to clean the kitchen, and now she found herself alone, enveloped in the silence of this big, sprawling house. Most nights she found solace in the quiet, but tonight she wandered around restlessly, not quite ready to turn in, not quite sure what she wanted to do.

Storm's loud whinnies carried into the house. Her ears perked up to the ruckus in the corral, and she put on her jacket and walked outside to investigate. She came to the corral in time to see Storm kicking up a big fuss. The stallion rounded the corral's perimeter at breakneck speed, snorting, his breaths shrill and labored. As Maddie approached the fence—his fence—he stopped short and stared at her.

"Hey Storm," she called out. "Are you restless, too?"

Storm continued to stare at her, edging up closer to the fence one careful step at a time. Maddie kept her eyes trained on Storm as she walked forward. "Don't be afraid."

Storm came closer still, until he stood three feet from the fence. "Thata, boy."

Maddie hummed a slow, easy tune, the melody catchy enough to gain the stallion's attention. She knew better than to force the situation. She stood her ground, not daring to move any further. Patience worked hand in hand with trust.

Low lying clouds and dim moonlight cast Storm in ominous shadows, making the noble horse seem somewhat sinister, but Maddie knew that wasn't the case at all. Storm wasn't tame by any horseman's standards. She wasn't a fool to think otherwise. He was prideful and intelligent and in time he would come around. "I know you," she said softly. "You think you're fooling me, but I know you."

Maddie headed back to the kitchen and grabbed a handful of sugar cubes. It was the oldest trick in the book, but the method was tried and true and had worked for her on countless occasions with feisty animals like Storm.

She set the cubes on top of the fence post, leaving Storm to wonder what she had done. "See you tomorrow, boy."

After entering the kitchen, Maddie stood by the window and waited. She stared at the obstinate horse for fifteen minutes and finally, her patience paid off. He approached the fence post and licked the sugar cubes clean.

"Thata boy." Her whisper floated on the air and a challenge emerged. She might not be able to get through to Trey Walker, but Storm was a different matter. Determined now, Maddie made herself a promise not to give up on the beautiful stallion. One way or another, she would gain Storm's trust.

"Night, Trey," Kit said, parking the car in front of the house. "Thanks for slumming it with me. I never thought I'd say this, but I can't wait until my wife gets home."

With one hand on the door handle, Trey smiled. "Hell, you're newly married. It ain't a sin to miss your wife. I didn't mind having drinks tonight. Sorta needed it myself."

Trey bounded out of the car and headed inside his house. He'd gone into town with Kit to have a few beers and listen to honky-tonk music at Tie-One-On, the local bar. Poor guy, he was smitten and missing his wife something fierce while she was visiting relatives in Houston.

Kit spent some time fending off the advances of hopeful females. Trey envied Kit's commitment to his wife. He envied the man his future, one filled with the love of a good woman and the promise of a family. Those things seemed so far out of Trey's reach that he'd put them completely out of his mind. He resigned himself to his life at 2 Hope, having been happy for most of his time here. That is, until one perky redhead came to live with him.

Tie-One-On was a place to help a man forget, a place to loosen up and have a good time. Half a dozen women had approached Trey tonight as well. He'd danced with a few, held them in his arms, but his mind kept going back to Maddie. Thoughts of her filled his head and he found himself sitting at the bar with his friend, amid a crowd of fun-loving people, feeling lonelier than he could ever remember.

Trey grabbed a beer from the refrigerator and headed to the parlor. He plopped down on the sofa, kicked up his boots on the table and clicked on the television set. He finally settled in when he found an old John Wayne movie.

The scent of raspberries drifted by and as he turned his head around, he saw Maddie making an about-face. "Maddie?"

"Oh, hi," she said, tightening her white robe around her.

"I didn't know you were out here. Don't let me disturb you."

"Can't sleep?"

"Not really. Guess I'm a little restless tonight."

Trey studied her appearance. Her face was washed clean of the little makeup she wore, her hair fell in waves around her shoulders as if she'd just brushed through it, and her bright green eyes held certain shyness. Of all the women Trey had spoken with tonight, of all the women he'd danced with and had briefly considered going home with, none of them appealed to him the way Maddie Brooks did.

Both of them were restless tonight.

Both needed companionship.

He knew better than to ask, but he asked anyway. "Do you like John Wayne?"

Maddie smiled. "Love him."

Trey patted the sofa next to him. "Pull up a seat."

A SHORT WHILE later after sharing a movie, a bowl of popcorn and a few lingering looks, Trey stretched out and continued to listen to Maddie's soft, soothing voice. "And so after my folks passed, my Grandma Mae and I moved to this little apartment in the heart of New York City. I knew immediately that I wouldn't do well in a big city. I needed space and freedom and animals. For one, you don't see too many animals in New York, unless you go to the zoo."

"So you knew early on that you wanted to work with animals?"

With a subtle tilt of her head, Maddie responded, "I know this sounds corny, but it wasn't so much what I knew inside. I was drawn to it, like a magnetic pull. I know what it means now when people say that they met their life's calling. Being a veterinarian was my calling. It's as if I had no choice in the matter." She smiled softly. "Does that make any sense?"

"More than you know," he said. Trey believed there were greater forces out there, working either for or against you. At this very moment there were forces working against him ever being with Maddie. It was something Trey just plain understood. "Sometimes, choices are taken from you." He scrubbed his jaw a moment. "It worked out for you, though. You're doing exactly what you were meant to do."

"And what about you, Trey? Are you doing what you're meant to do?"

Trey shrugged. "Ranching's in my blood, I suppose—2 Hope has been around a long, long time. We've had some rough patches, but we're hanging on."

"I'd love to know how 2 Hope got its name," she said. "Or is that one of the stories not fit for polite company?"

Maddie wiggled closer on the sofa, her robe parting slightly. Trey caught a glimpse of thin silky pajamas underneath. Her exposed skin shone like polished porcelain and that necklace she wore caught his eye. The damn thing dangled right smack in between her breasts.

Trey drew in oxygen and glanced back up to her face. He wasn't immune to her wholesome charm, not in the least. He figured he was better off looking into pretty green eyes than lusting over soft, creamy skin.

"Now that's a story I *can* tell you," he said. "Legend has it that my great-great-granddaddy was down on his luck when he arrived in Hope Wells. Didn't take him long to figure out what he wanted. A ranch and my great-great-grandmother. Only problem was, my grandmother was Rachel Hope, the daughter of the richest man in town. And Will Walker didn't have two nickels to rub together. But he found a way. He won the ranch in a poker game and shortly after," Trey said, with a smile he couldn't hide, "he won Rachel. Seems my grandfather's opponent in that famous poker game had drawn a full house. He made no bones about it. He'd told everyone what he held in his hand. Poor old Will thought he was done for, all he had was a pair of two's. Was too much to hope for—another pair of two's, but dang it all, if he didn't draw them. He won the hand with four of a kind—four two's."

Maddie smiled, a distant, winsome expression on her face. "Two Hope. That's a lovely story, Trey. It must be nice knowing about your ancestors. You have such a deep foundation here, a sense of belonging."

"When things get rough around here, and I think I'm ready to chuck it all, I recall the way the ranch got started."

"That's admirable, Trey."

"There's nothing admirable about it."

"What do you mean?"

Trey shook his head. He hadn't meant to blurt that out, yet he felt he didn't deserve her compliment. He wasn't that noble. Lately he'd been feeling resentful—hating the traits he'd inherited that made him lack a sense of commitment. If Maddie only knew how many times he'd been tempted to sell off the ranch, to rid himself of the headaches and make a fresh start somewhere. If she only knew how much he'd wanted to be more solid, more stable. He'd messed up enough in one lifetime. He had bad genes to thank for that. His father, and his father before him, hadn't set the best example. Neither of those men were anything like Will Walker. Will had had staying power. Will Walker had had the guts to see things through.

"Nothing. Forget it, Maddie."

"But—"

Loud howling coming from the barn interrupted Maddie's thoughts. She stopped speaking to listen. "Sounds like Maggie and Toby."

Trey sat upright and listened carefully to the barking dogs. "Something's got them upset. I'd best go check."

Maddie rose quickly. "I'm coming, too."

They raced outside toward the barn, Trey searching the area with sharp, probing eyes. He wished he'd thought to grab his rifle as he yanked the barn door open. The barking simmered some. Maddie swooped down next to Toby, the black-and-white border collie she'd been nursing from a car accident.

"Oh no. Toby's ripped open his stitches. He's bleeding, Trey."

"What can I do?"

"Stay with him while I get the supplies I need."

Maddie rose but Trey grabbed her arm. "Be careful. It might have been a coyote scratching to get inside. He's probably long gone by now, but I'm not sure."

"I'll be careful."

Trey stood and watched Maddie enter her office space, keeping a vigilant eye out for whatever culprit caused the animals to get into such a ruckus. He only relaxed when he saw her running back toward him, her arms filled with the supplies she needed.

"Okay, Toby," she said softly to the injured collie. "Looks like you're not going home tomorrow, after all."

An hour later, Trey escorted an exhausted Maddie to her bedroom door. Together, they'd worked on Toby, Trey holding the dog while Maddie administered to the freshly opened wound. Maddie wouldn't leave until the dog finally calmed and had fallen back asleep.

"Hazards of the barn," Trey offered by way of apology. "We get all sorts of wild animals out here."

Maddie shrugged. "I think Toby will heal just fine. And using the barn to practice is a far cry better than having no place at all."

"True enough," Trey said. "But maybe we should change the name from 2 Hope to Last Chance Ranch."

"After that wonderful story you told me, don't you dare." Maddie reached for Trey's arm, her subtle touch searing his skin under his shirt. She'd shed her bathrobe in the barn, and both had been too caught up with their task to notice, but now, Trey noticed. Her soft, silky tank top left little to the imagination; her perfect breasts stretched the material in ways that made his mouth go dry. And her cotton drawers, decorated with blue and white clouds, hugged her hips below her navel, accentuated her delicate curves. "I really do appreciate being able to practice here, Trey. I know it isn't the perfect situation, but I'm grateful for everything. Including your help tonight."

Trey wasn't sure who'd received the most benefit tonight. His evening had livened up the moment Maddie had entered the parlor. He'd been unsettled and lonely and as soon as he'd seen Maddie everything had changed. In truth, Trey couldn't remember having a more satisfying and enjoyable evening.

"I'm glad to help out."

"Thank you," she said, staring into his eyes.

He stared back, captivated by this pretty, petite woman. She was warm and kind and sweet, and Trey realized he wanted more than a bed partner in Maddie, he wanted to be her friend.

He bent down and touched his lips to hers softly. "Good night, Dr. Maddie."

"Good night, Trey," she whispered, leaning her head against the door.

Trey backed up quickly, and turned away from the longing he witnessed in her eyes, the surprised smile on her face. He turned away from the tempting woman, turning away from every single instinct calling him back.

"DAMN IT ALL, Uncle Monty."

Trey cursed so darn loud from the other room, Maddie nearly spilled her morning coffee. She sat in the kitchen, reading the newspaper, trying to fully awaken after getting in so late last night. It had been worth the lack of sleep. One of the best evenings of her life. And then, contrary to what Trey had preached, he'd given her another kiss.

But this kiss seemed different, less passionate, but somehow more intimate. As if they'd somehow created a bond. Maddie didn't believe Trey had been playing with her heart. The way he'd kissed her had been innocent and spontaneous, as unplanned as Texas heat, making it all the more special.

"Turn the water *off*, Uncle Monty." Trey shouted to his uncle in a grumble erupting from his throat.

Her curiosity heightened, Maddie headed into the smaller bathroom where all the noise was coming from. She found

Trey facing a broken out wall, holding together a galvanized pipe with both hands, trying to keep the leak from sprouting again. "*Off,*" he shouted out the window.

Maddie giggled.

Trey turned in surprise, releasing his hands slightly.

Water rained out, spurting him in the face and shoulders. Within seconds, Trey Walker was drenched, the leaky pipe gushing out until finally and apparently, his Uncle Monty had turned the water *off.*

Trey's hair hung in wet clumps around his head. Water plastered his T-shirt to his chest and the top of his blue jeans were saturated.

Maddie let out a belly laugh at the rugged man who now looked like a scruffy pup. "Having trouble?" she asked, with a grin.

"You might say that," Trey growled. "My uncle doesn't seem to know the difference between 'on' and 'off' and why the heck are you laughing?"

Maddie turned to the cabinet to get Trey a towel. "Because you look like—"

But when Maddie turned back around, she found Trey removing his T-shirt, the material stretching over his smooth, wet skin in one quick movement. He tossed the shirt into the bathtub and ran a hand through his hair, slicking back the dark strands until he looked better than a *GQ* model in blue jeans.

Maddie swallowed, trying to keep her expression from

faltering. She'd seen Trey shirtless before and admittedly it had been glorious, but he hadn't been wet, with droplets falling from his hair onto his shoulders, with water licking at the scattering of hairs on his chest until a puddle developed in his navel.

Goodness. There wasn't a more appealing man on the face of the Earth.

"Like what?" he asked, his growl simmering, a curious expression taking over.

Maddie balled up the towel and approached him. "Like a mangy old mutt I once treated," she fibbed, holding her breath as she dabbed at his powerfully built, solid chest.

He stared at her, his voice holding a hint of disbelief. "An old mutt?"

She nodded, continuing to dab at him. "Uh-huh. Poor thing had fallen into the river."

Maddie stifled a noisy gasp. Touching Trey this intimately was doing her in. She held up well considering that she was mere minutes from jumping the man's bones. "All finished," she said, thrusting the towel into his arms. Trey let the towel drop to the ground between them and as she took a step back, he grabbed her wrists, tugging her gently closer.

He grinned mischievously, "Not quite."

Before Maddie knew it, Trey reached down into the rain bucket used to catch the leak, and splashed her with handful after handful of water. "Trey!"

Maddie backed away and stared down at her fully

drenched wet clothes.

This time, he laughed. "The mangy mutt wanted a companion." Then he came closer, grabbing a dry towel. "Here," he said, approaching her. "Fair is fair." He dabbed at her face, taking care to dry her cheeks, mouth, and chin. Then he sent a searing look past her shoulders. "If you toss off your blouse, I'll do your chest," he offered softly. "Just like you did mine."

Fleeting, forbidden thoughts of Trey patting her naked body dry flashed in her head and she realized she'd never had a better offer in her life. She grabbed the towel out of his hands, "Not a chance, cowboy."

Trey threw his head back and laughed even more, stepping back and away from her.

"Well, what have we here?" Monty Walker asked, catching the two of them red-handed. Guilty, Maddie glanced at the floor. "Hi there, Monty."

Trey still had laughter in his voice when he volunteered, "Maddie was teaching me the finer points of plumbing."

Monty glanced from Trey to Maddie. "That so?" Then he added, "Well, somebody's got to." He winked at Maddie. "The man's an expert horseman, but doesn't know diddly about fixing a leak."

Trey stood next to Monty, putting an arm around his shoulder. "At least I know which way is . . . off?"

"Oh, that. I was just funning with you."

Trey's expression went bleak the second he realized what

the older man had done. Maddie giggled again.

"The woman loves to laugh at me," Trey said to Monty. "But I'll get back at her when I cook dinner tonight."

"Oh," Maddie said, realizing she'd forgotten to tell Trey she wouldn't be home tonight. "Guess I'm getting off easy then. I won't be home for dinner."

Trey nodded. "A late-night house call?"

Maddie shook her head. "Not tonight. I have a date."

Chapter Five

TREY SAT IN a booth at the Hungry Wrangler Cafe with his uncle Monty and his cousin, Jack. He and Jack were about the same age and had been more like brothers than cousins while growing up. Trey pushed around his food on the plate, while the other two ate with gusto.

"Ain't you hungry, boy?" Uncle Monty asked, eyeing Trey's half-eaten steak. The retired sheriff of Hope Wells pulled no punches. He spoke his mind. Most of the time, Trey enjoyed his uncle's antics, but tonight he wasn't in the mood. Common courtesy and a true measure of gratefulness had Trey offering to treat his uncle to dinner. He'd worked most of the morning and half the afternoon fixing that doggone leak.

"Have at it," he said, sliding the plate his way. "Guess I'm not that hungry after all."

Jack glanced up from his meal and cast him an inquisitive look. "You sick or something?"

Jack Walker wore his uniform proudly. He'd just been reelected as sheriff of Hope Wells. First Monty, then Jack—between the two they had five decades of law enforcement under their belts.

"No, I'm not sick, just not very hungry." He sipped his iced tea.

Uncle Monty grunted as he stabbed at Trey's steak. "The man's lovesick, if you ask me."

Jack's brows rose, his expression none too subtle. "That pretty little Dr. Maddie getting under your skin?"

Uncle Monty didn't give him time to answer. He chimed in, "Under his skin? The boy wants her under his *sheets*. Should have seen his face when she told him she had a date tonight."

"Turned green, did he?" Jack jested.

Trey slammed down his glass. They were having too much fun at his expense. "Enough!"

Monty and Jack looked at one another and then burst out laughing. Trey waited a beat for their laughter to die down, "You through now?"

Both men nodded. "Good, because I'll say this only once. Nothing's going on between Maddie and me. We made a business deal and we're sticking to it."

Uncle Monty lifted his fork and pointed it his way. "Yeah, monkey business. Looked like you two were having a wet T-shirt contest when I walked in this morning."

Trey ground his teeth. "That wouldn't have happened if you had turned the water *off*."

Monty scratched behind his ear. "She sure is cute."

Jack nodded. "Is she seeing anyone in particular?"

Trey shook his head. "I don't know. We don't discuss things like that." But he was dying to know what lucky son-of-a-gun was on her dance card tonight.

"Maybe I should give her a call," Jack said, his expression thoughtful.

"You don't own any animals," Trey reminded.

Jack smiled. "Maybe it's time I get some."

Trey glared at his cousin. The friendly competition they'd had ever since they were young boys, just got old. He wouldn't put a name to how he was feeling tonight but he wasn't about to let Jack ring his bell. He shrugged. "Fine by me."

"It really cost you to say that, didn't it?" Jack asked with a big grin. But before Trey could make a denial, Jack added, all manner of jesting aside, "Look, I'm not going to call her, but if you're interested, I wouldn't hesitate. Maddie's got a lot going for her and some other guy is bound to discover that soon."

"She deserves to be happy," Trey stated.

"Dang it, Trey. You're holding on to that Walker Curse thing, aren't you?"

Trey stared his cousin down. Jack had no idea how many women had been hurt by the Walker men in his family. His cousin had no idea how bad Trey was at commitment. He had no idea how strongly he felt about this subject. Trey's mind was made up. There was no changing it. "You come from a family who uphold the law. Your heritage is different than mine, cousin. I come from a long line of men who break hearts. True, we have the same grandfather, but his traits didn't seem to rub off on you."

"We don't know that yet."

Jack was true blue. Jack would never let down anyone he loved. Trey was sure of his cousin. "I know you. You're as loyal as they come. And besides, you both have it all wrong. Yes, I'm in a sour mood tonight, but not because of anything having to do with Maddie."

"Then why?" Jack asked.

Trey frowned. "Because your father told me this afternoon that eventually, sooner than later, I'm going to have to replace all the old galvanized pipes at the house with copper. Seems my plumbing is somewhat out of date."

Monty grinned, his gray-blue eyes twinkling. "Hell boy, that's what we've been trying to tell you all along."

MADDIE STOOD BY Storm's corral, eyeing the stallion in the moonlight. She'd noticed once again that Trey wasn't home, giving her the perfect chance to work with the feisty horse. She'd been sneaking out here for the past four nights, ever since her dinner date with Caroline and little Annabelle last Saturday night. And during those nights, Storm had been guarded but every so often Maddie would see a spark of change, a subtle softening in Storm's demeanor that had encouraged Maddie to continue to gain the horse's trust.

Maddie had used treats, but she also depended on her innate ability to read animals, and she sensed that Storm was getting ready to accept her. Each night, Maddie approached with caution. Storm, too, approached warily. Last night, Storm had actually taken the sugar cubes from her hand.

Tonight, she merely stood by the fence and watched as Storm pranced, snorted, and then raced around the perimeter of the corral, all the while communicating with Maddie in a language she truly did understand.

When he finished his exercise, he stopped and stared. Then, ever so slowly, he approached the fence where Maddie stood. "Are you glad to see me again?" she asked softly. "Well, I'm sure glad to see you."

He came right up to the fence and Maddie stepped on the bottom rung to reach him. "Hey, boy," she whispered into the still night and reached her hand out to stroke his ink-black mane. Then bravely, and only because she sensed he was ready, she ran her hand smoothly down his snout.

The horse lifted his head in a quick movement, but he didn't back away. Maddie stroked him once more, continuing to speak to him in a soft, soothing tone.

When Maddie heard Trey's truck in the distance, she jumped down from the fence and said farewell to Storm. "See you tomorrow night." Unable to make her escape into the house without seeming obvious, she stood by the front porch as the truck came to a stop a short distance away. To her surprise, a pretty young woman who was at least six months pregnant exited the driver's seat. Trey got out of the passenger's side, and the woman strolled over to him and reached for his hand. They stood there speaking quietly for a few minutes.

Maddie's heart took an elevator ride down to her toes. Her gut clenched involuntarily and feelings she thought she had under control emerged with raw clarity. Seeing Trey with another woman, one he might have an involvement with, knocked her for a giant-size loop. All sorts of images popped into her head, and none of the scenarios she came up with helped to ease her mind. She didn't know who this woman was and she decided she couldn't bear to know. Not tonight. Not with the realization that Trey hadn't come home for dinner in the past four nights.

Maddie made a move to enter the house, but the woman caught sight of her and called out, "Hi there."

Maddie turned to find the woman heading her way, with Trey beside her. "Hello."

The woman was even prettier up close, a young Texas lady through and through, with deep blue eyes and long blond hair. "I've been meaning to get out here to say hello. Sorry to hear about your office burning down. My name is Brittany Fuller. I'm a friend of Trey's."

"Nice to meet you, Brittany. I'm Maddie Brooks."

"I know. Trey's always talking about you. He says you're a real good veterinarian."

Maddie glanced at Trey who appeared darn uncomfortable, his tanned face taking on color. She shrugged. "I love working with animals."

"I had to drive Trey home," the pregnant woman offered, smiling at him. "No offense, Trey. But you're one stubborn man." Then she explained to Maddie, "He hurt his hand working on my baby's new room. A beam of wood fell down and when Trey tried to catch it he got splintered up."

For the first time since he'd walked up, Maddie took a really good look at Trey. And suddenly she understood the expression on his face. Pain. She peered down at his right hand. "Oh! That doesn't look good at all."

Gently she reached for his hand to get a better look. Holding his hand in her palm, she noted where five or six long splinters had been hastily removed, the hand puffy, swollen and red.

"Paul and I wouldn't let Trey drive home. Though he did argue some."

Maddie glanced up. "Paul?"

"My husband. He'll be here in a minute. Paul and Trey have been friends just about forever, I guess. And when Paul hurt his back a few days ago, Trey came over first thing to help finish up the room." She patted her rounded belly. "Our baby will be here before you know it."

"Oh," Maddie said, dumbfounded. This was almost too much information to digest all at once. All of her initial suspicions about Trey and this woman were unfounded.

She'd let jealousy rule out over reason. This woman and her husband were his friends. Trey had been doing a good deed and Brittany had driven him home because he'd gotten hurt. "Well, congratulations on the baby. Do you know what you're having?"

She shook her head. "We want to be surprised."

"That's nice. I wouldn't want to know, either," she said, realizing this was the first time she'd really given any thought to having a child. Suddenly it was clear that she did want children. And she too wanted to be surprised. "I hope your husband's back injury isn't too serious."

"The doctor told him to rest up a bit, but Paul's a stubborn one, too, and wouldn't stop, so Trey decided to come over and do the heavy work. Wouldn't take no for an answer. Even my thrown-together suppers didn't scare him away."

"Your suppers are delicious, Brit," Trey said immediately.

She smiled softly. "But now *you're* hurt, too."

"It's not that bad."

Maddie disagreed, "It looks kind of bad, Trey. Maybe you should see a doctor."

He twisted his mouth, lifting his hand up. "For this? No way."

"I was hoping . . . " Brittany said to Maddie, a look of concern on her face.

"Of course," Maddie said instantly. "I'll patch him up."

Trey shook his head. "There's nothing to patch up."

"Yes, there is," both women chorused.

And before Trey could argue, Brittany's husband pulled up in a white SUV. "Looks like my ride's here" she said, and after Maddie had been introduced to Paul, Brittany got into the car and waved farewell.

Maddie turned back to Trey.

"There's nothing to patch up," he said stubbornly.

"SIT DOWN, TREY, and don't be a baby," Maddie said softly, pointing to the kitchen chair. She'd gathered up her medical supplies and was ready.

"I don't need any doctoring, Maddie," he said again, but the woman wouldn't take no for an answer.

She stared at him with expectant eyes, so pretty, so dewy-grass-green, so *determined.* She'd accused him of packing a wallop the other day, but she was guilty of the same. One look at her sweetly concerned face had him sitting, obeying like a wayward puppy at obedience school.

Trey didn't want her to doctor him. He didn't want her anywhere near him. She was too much of a temptation, too much of a distraction. He'd been trying to keep his distance, but living under the same roof with her made it damn difficult. Every time he got close to Maddie, he would do something stupid, like taking her into his arms and kissing her.

Maddie set a bowl of warm water down on the table then took a seat close to him and the subtle scent of raspberries wafted by. She lifted his hand and set it into the water. "We'll let it soak for a while."

She opened his hand carefully and with delicate care massaged his fingers. She stroked gently, easing soreness and bringing back circulation. It felt good, damn good. Trey closed his eyes and let the sensations run through his body. Maddie had a great touch. Maybe too great, he thought, because circulation began to build in another area of his body as well. He cursed under his breath.

"Does it hurt?" she asked immediately, lifting her head from the task.

"No."

"I thought I heard you groan."

Trey kept silent.

"I'm going to dry your hand, put on an antiseptic and wrap it."

"I can't work with it wrapped."

Maddie smiled. "So you'll take the day off tomorrow."

"I don't take days off, Maddie. Not when I'm running the ranch on a shoestring."

Maddie shook her head, her doctoring instincts taking hold. She spoke in a stern voice, one Trey had never heard before. "You're lucky you don't need stitches, Trey. Those wood bits ripped your hand up real good going in, and whoever yanked them out ripped your hand up again."

Again, Trey was silent.

Maddie read straight through his poker face.

"Let me guess, you're the one who pulled out those splinters."

"Good guess."

She sighed. "Trey."

Trey leaned back in the chair, crossing his leg over his knee, and watched as Maddie attended to his hand. With her head bent to the task, Trey stared at her silky hair falling in soft waves onto her shoulders. She held him so carefully, mindful when the antiseptic stung and lifting apologetic eyes his way. She took gauze out of her medical bag, placing it over the wound then wrapped his hand with surgical tape, taking her time, using her skills as a healer.

Whenever he looked at Maddie, he saw his future. But the vision was false, a deception of the mind, because Trey wasn't the man for her. She deserved someone she could trust not to wound her gentle soul. He chalked up these unwelcome sentiments to being around Paul and Brittany all week. With the new baby coming, their excitement had rubbed off on him. He found himself longing for the same, a wife and family. And being with Kit wasn't much help, either. That man was so doggone smitten with his new wife he barely spoke a sentence without mentioning her name.

Trey knew people with successful relationships. That's all it was—this *wanting* he'd been experiencing lately. But his father's words haunted him daily. And Trey had vowed not to make those same mistakes. Trey was smart enough to realize that *wanting* and *having* were two different things. He wasn't cut out for family life. He'd tried that once and had failed miserably.

"Promise me something, Trey," Maddie said as she finished up bandaging him. "You won't go busting up this hand I worked so hard on tonight. You won't injure yourself again." She held his wrapped hand in both of hers and stared at him with softness in her eyes.

"Hell, Maddie," he whispered, leaning close, beckoned by her caring nature and her sweet, tentative smile. "When you ask me like that, there isn't anything I wouldn't promise you."

Maddie leaned in also, coming dangerously close, their eyes meeting. "There isn't?" she asked breathlessly.

Raspberry sweet and red-haired sexy, Trey had a mind to kiss her again, the need so strong that he couldn't pull away. He stared at her heart-shaped mouth, glossy and full, parting slightly. He wanted to lift her out of the chair, put her onto his lap and brush his lips over hers until kissing wasn't enough.

Hell, who was he kidding? He wanted to lay her down on the kitchen table and . . .

And then the shrill ring of the phone brought him back to reality.

Trey jerked back in his chair. Idiot. He'd almost made

another mistake and although it would take his body a moment to adjust, he was glad for the interruption. He bounded up and answered the wall phone by the refrigerator. "Hello."

A few seconds later, he brought the receiver over to Maddie, stretching out the long cord. "Do you know a Nick Spencer?"

Maddie's face beamed with joy. She stood up, practically standing on her toes. "It's Nick? Really?"

"That's what he said." Trey handed her the phone.

"Nick, I can't believe it's you." Maddie twirled the cord around her fingers. "How did you find me?"

Trey walked out the back door and into the night air, to give Maddie some privacy and to cool himself off. He told himself over and over he was glad he hadn't kissed her again. He told himself he was glad Maddie had a personal life outside of her work. He told himself he was glad this guy Nick had called, interrupting the wild fantasy he had entertained.

He glanced down at his bandaged hand, flexing his fingers and feeling no pain. He took a deep crisp breath, realizing that most of all, he was glad he hadn't made any promises to Maddie.

Promises that he couldn't keep.

Chapter Six

D RAWING A BREATH, she knocked on the hotel room door at the Cactus Inn. She was looking forward to seeing Nick, the friend she hadn't seen in the year since she'd moved to Hope Wells. They'd gone to UC Davis together, Nick receiving his DVM two years before she'd graduated. But she and Nick had stayed in touch while he worked as an intern in Fresno, California. He'd made quite a name for himself in the field of veterinary medicine, having saved the life of a K-9 from the Faithful Partner police-dog program. The dog had taken a bullet for his human partner, and Nick had worked relentlessly to save his life.

He'd become something of a local hero then, but that hadn't slowed him down. Nick went on to join an international symposium on bioterrorism, and he gave his time to worthy animal-related endeavors. In short, Nick was brilliant, and Maddie considered herself lucky to be his good friend.

Maddie smiled as he opened the door. "Hi, Nick."

Nick grinned immediately and opened his arms. She stepped into his friendly and warm embrace. "Maddie."

Maddie pulled away to look into his sky-blue eyes. "You look wonderful. I can't believe you're here."

He had blond good looks and charm to spare. Clean-cut as they come, his look never changed. Today, as usual, he wore a crisp button-down shirt and dark pleated trousers "I'm here to see my best friend."

"*Best* friend? We haven't spoken in months. I was beginning to think you'd forgotten about me way out here in Texas."

"Nope, I couldn't forget you. I've been busy, Maddie. That's why I'm here. We have to talk. I have a proposition for you."

"You came all the way out to Hope Wells to proposition me?"

He took hold of her hand. "Yes, I did. Listen, I know you don't have more than an hour or so with me this morning before you have to get back to work, and I'd like to see something of the town. Show me around, and we'll talk tonight, over dinner?"

"A proposition *and* a dinner invitation? How can a girl refuse?"

"You can't and you won't, I hope. But I don't want to get ahead of myself here." He stopped smiling and squeezed her hand. "I'd like to see where your office was, Maddie. I came as soon as I heard the news. Thank God you and the animals weren't hurt."

"Yes, we were fortunate. And I have Trey Walker to

thank for taking us all in."

"He's the man you're living with?" There was nothing suspect in his tone, yet Maddie felt the need to clarify her cowboy contract.

"Yes. It's a business arrangement until my office can be rebuilt. I'm renting out a room at the ranch and practicing out of his old barn."

Nick nodded. "You always were enterprising, Maddie. Good for you."

Nick had been Maddie's biggest fan while in school. He'd always admired her dedication to her work and her special talent with animals. They'd gotten along great at the university and she was glad to see that their camaraderie hadn't faded. "Thanks, Nick."

"Are you ready to show me Hope Wells?"

"I'm absolutely ready."

Nick took her hand in his as they left the hotel room.

TREY HELD A pair of aces in his left hand, the best you can draw in Texas Hold 'Em. He glanced at his opponents, Kit, Jack, Monty and two of his ranch hands, keeping his poker face. None of his opponents looked too happy.

"I'm all in," he said, pushing his chip stack into the center of the kitchen table. Taking special care with his bandaged hand, he congratulated himself for obeying

Maddie's orders. He hadn't done a lick of work today.

The men grumbled and only one player decided to call the bet. Jack tallied up Trey's stack and pushed an equal amount of chips into the pot. All in all, the pot size equaled less than ten dollars—playing with nickel and dime chips didn't allow for too much loss. A good thing too, since Trey's funds were meant for essentials such as hay and feed and household expenses. But he didn't want the family tradition to die. The Walker clan had been playing poker since Will Walker's days.

Trey turned over his two cards at the same time Jack flipped his over. Jack held a pair of sevens and so far, Trey's aces had him beat.

The dealer flopped three of the five community cards onto the table and they didn't help either player's hand. With Trey going all in, Jack couldn't raise the bet, so the fourth community card was dealt and again, no help.

"Come on," Trey said, ready to taste victory when the river card was flipped. Trey had a solid chance of winning. It was all about percentages and they were greatly in his favor. Hell, he'd waited a long time for a hand like this.

But before Monty drew the last card, Maddie's voice stole into the room. "Hi guys. Just wanted to say good night and have fun."

Maddie stood at the kitchen doorway and all eyes fell on her.

"C'mon in here, girl, and let us see you proper-like," Uncle Monty encouraged.

"I don't want to interrupt."

"Ah hell, it's just our usual monthly poker game. You're not interrupting."

Trey took his eyes off his cards to glance at Maddie as she stepped into the room and his breath hitched in his throat. Damn.

She looked beautiful and dressed to destroy in a tight, cleavage-spilling dress that matched the jade green hue of her eyes. The skimpy dress left nothing to the imagination in the leg department either. He tried to recall if he'd ever seen her in anything but jeans, but he figured he would've surely remembered those gorgeous legs. His gaze drifted down to her dainty feet encased in three-inch strappy black heels. Hell, a man could fantasize for days about those shoes alone.

The whole Maddie package made his mouth go dry.

"Wow, you look great," Jack said, his eyes nearly bulging out of his head.

"You can interrupt any time," Kit said with a wink.

The others added compliments as well, one man letting loose a long, low wolf whistle.

"Got a hot date?" Uncle Monty asked, a bit too gleefully for Trey's way of thinking.

"No, just dinner with an old friend," Maddie replied, her face flushed with color.

Why was in hell was she blushing? Was it the idea of her date with that Nick Spencer guy that colored her pretty cheeks?

"Nick and I go way back," she said. "We went to college together. He was passing through town and stopped to say hello."

"Hell, no one just passes through Hope Wells," Uncle Monty advised. "That man did some zigzagging to get to you."

Maddie chuckled.

Trey frowned. This morning, he'd driven past her burned-down office on his way to the grocery and had seen the two of them, hand in hand, peering at what was left of Maddie's veterinary office. She'd had her head on his shoulder, and it certainly didn't appear that they were just friends. Hell, the image of the two of them like that had put him in a sour mood all day.

"Trey, don't you think Maddie looks pretty tonight?" Uncle Monty prodded.

Trey ground his teeth. He knew what Uncle Monty was up to, but he'd call his bluff; this was, after all, *poker* night. Trey pulled out his chair and stood up. He walked over to Maddie and stared deep into her eyes. "I hope your date appreciates how beautiful you are, inside and out," he said, taking her hand. "C'mon, I'll walk you out."

"Okay," Maddie agreed. "Goodnight everyone."

"Have a great time," Uncle Monty said.

The others also bid her farewell, and Trey guided her toward the front door with her hand clasped in his. It felt so natural, so right, as if this should be their date, as if she'd dressed up special just for him, as if they had a wonderful evening to look forward to. And if things were different, Trey would take her hand and steal her away so no other man could hold her, no other man could touch her.

But Trey had to let her go. He released her hand. "Enjoy your evening out, Maddie. Have fun tonight."

"Thank you. I always enjoy being with Nick."

That comment slashed through his gut. Trey nodded and Maddie took a step toward her truck, but then she spun back around and stared into his eyes. "Trey, do you really mean it?"

Trey stood ramrod still. He couldn't believe Maddie had called him on this. Her expression held something akin to hope. He couldn't breathe, couldn't think. Emotions washed over him, fast and furiously, and he could only hear what his heart told him. Did he mean it? Did he want her to enjoy her evening with another man? Hell, no. But he couldn't admit that to Maddie, and right now he couldn't lie to her either. They stared at each other for a long, drawn-out moment, his poker face hopefully back in place.

Uncle Monty called out, "Trey, boy, you playing poker or courting the lady?"

Trey lifted one side of his mouth. "I'd better get back to the game."

"Go," she said, "they're waiting. And Trey," she added, just as he was about to head back to the game, "I'm glad you took care with your hand today."

She turned her back and walked away.

Trey watched her climb into her truck and pull away as an ache gnawed through his stomach. He walked back into the kitchen and stood over his poker hand. "Let's see that last card," he said to the dealer.

The dealer turned over a seven of hearts.

Jack hit three of a kind, his three sevens beating out Trey's two aces.

Trey slumped into his seat. "Boy, I didn't see that coming."

"Sorry, Trey," Jack said, hauling in all of his chips. "Looks like you're through."

"That's poker for you," Uncle Monty said bluntly. "It's a lot like life. You don't see it coming, until it's too late."

AFTER THE GAME ended, Trey grabbed empty beer bottles from the table and tossed them in the trash. Only Jack and Uncle Monty remained at the house.

"Too bad you came out the loser tonight, cousin," Jack stated, putting poker chips back in their holder.

Trey shrugged. He didn't give a damn about his poker loss tonight. It baffled him why that was, until an image of Maddie standing in the moonlight, looking like everything he'd ever wanted in a woman, popped into his head.

"I'll get you next month," he said to Jack.

His cousin's mouth twisted. "I wasn't talking about the game, Trey."

Uncle Monty stood next to him and laid a hand on his shoulder. "You didn't see that hand coming cause you weren't looking, boy. The same holds true in life. You think you're holding a winning hand and then someone comes along with one better. Before you know it, the game's lost. That's what Jack's talking about."

Trey blew out a breath. "You're talking about Maddie."

Monty looked him straight in the eyes. "You took a risk tonight. You went all-in on a hand you believed would win. Sometimes you've got to do that right here." He pressed a finger into Trey's chest, just above his heart. "Go *all in*, boy. Don't lose that girl."

"Lose her?"

"Yeah. You've got to ask yourself, what would be worse, winning that girl or losing her forever?"

"You're forgetting that I took a risk on that last hand and came out the loser anyway."

"Ah, but at least you gave it your best shot." Monty's smile reached eyes. "Remember, if you don't play, you can't possibly win. Get in the game, Trey. Play the percentages. Judging by the way that little lady looks at you, I'd say you're the odds-on favorite. She's worth the gamble."

But Maddie would be the one taking the bigger risk, because sure as the sun sets, Trey would break her heart. And that was a chance he wasn't willing to take.

LATER THAT NIGHT Maddie pulled through the gates of 2 Hope Ranch, her mind spinning from her dinner with Nick. He'd really thrown her off balance with his proposition, giving her a whole lot to think about. It had been all she *could* think about tonight, and as she traveled the road toward 2 Hope and Trey, she tossed around all of her options. She wondered about her future here in Hope Wells comparing it to the marvelous opportunity awaiting her with Nick.

A fleeting sense of belonging struck her as she parked the truck by Trey's ranch house. She'd come to think of this place as home. She'd settled in quite nicely here, enjoying the peace of ranch life. She was surrounded by green pastures and solid earth. The scents rising to her nostrils spoke of healthy animals and straw and, yes, even cow dung.

And Trey. *He* was here.

She liked the thought of coming home to him.

He'd looked at her differently tonight, as though he'd really *seen* the woman that she was. She didn't mistake the hunger in his eyes or the way his gaze raked over her body with appreciation and desire.

Maddie's heart started racing the moment he'd taken her hand to walk her outside. She'd thought he'd stop her from going out with Nick and when he didn't, her hope of having a solid relationship with him shattered.

Was she fooling herself thinking that 2 Hope was really her home? Trey Walker wasn't the man waiting for her. This was a temporary business arrangement, a handshake contract that served both her and Trey well. There was no use holding on to sentimental thoughts.

Maddie climbed down from the truck and glanced at Storm's corral. He spotted her and trotted right up to the fence.

Progress.

Maddie smiled and called softly to the horse, "I'll be right back."

She tiptoed into the darkened house through the back door and proceeded to her bedroom. All was quiet, Trey having probably turned in hours ago. Still, Maddie made little noise as she undressed, taking off her dress and slipping out of her heels silently. She couldn't pass up this chance to work with Storm. He'd been on her mind quite a bit lately. Maddie enjoyed the private time she spent with the stallion. She found getting to know the intricacies of the animal's spirit as rewarding as the act of healing.

Once dressed in her regular work clothes—jeans and a denim shirt—she headed outside, mindful not to wake Trey. There was a part of her that wanted to surprise him with Storm's progress, but she also worried that Trey wouldn't approve of these late-night tests of will.

One look at Storm and Maddie knew the horse was nearly ready. Without qualms, she opened the corral gate and entered Storm's territory. They had a staring bout for a few seconds before Storm allowed her approach. "Hey there," she cooed softly. "It's just me."

Maddie stroked the horse's mane, then moved her hand to his snout. Fearlessly she came around to face him and looked up into his eyes as she continued to stroke him. "You're beginning to trust me, Storm. That's a good thing, boy." She reached inside her jeans and handed the stallion half a dozen sugar cubes. "Or are you charming me just for these treats?"

The stallion gobbled them down without hesitation. "One hundred percent male," Maddie said on a soft chuckle. "But let's see if you really trust me."

And Maddie headed to the barn for a lead rope.

TREY CLOSED THE door to his Chevy Silverado and entered the house. His first thoughts were of Maddie. He missed seeing her. He'd been at Paul and Brittany's every night since poker night, working long hours on the baby's room. Thanks to Maddie's ministrations, his hand had healed up real nicely even with all the hammering he'd been doing lately. Now, the nursery was officially finished, and a great sense of accomplishment washed over him.

Trey grabbed a beer from the refrigerator, twisted off the cap and brought the bottle to his lips. Gazing out the window to a night black as pitch, he slugged down half the contents in one thirsty gulp.

As a thank you to everyone who'd pitched in on the baby's new nursery, Brittany insisted on throwing a small party. She'd included Maddie and had given Trey direct instructions to present her with the hand-written invitation. Trey knew better than to argue with a pregnant lady, especially one determined to make a new friend.

He finished the rest of his beer and strode to Maddie's bedroom reaching into his breast pocket for the invitation. The door was open and he called to her. "Maddie? You in there?"

She didn't answer. He peeked inside the darkened room and called her name again. He was met with silence. She had to be somewhere on the grounds. He'd seen her truck parked by the house when he'd pulled up. Fleeting thoughts of her with that Nick guy, immediately vanished. Her friend had left town a few days ago.

Trey walked outside and headed toward the barn. Every night, Maddie checked in on her animals before bed. All was still and quiet as he approached the barn doors. Then a howling in the distance disturbed the peace. The hairs on the back of his neck rose. Instincts Trey relied on for most of his life told him something was wrong. His boots ate dry earth, his eyes focused and sharp as he scoured the grounds for signs of trouble. Then his gaze hit upon something disturbing.

Storm's corral was empty.

"Damn it." A cold snap of fear emerged. His hands fisted tight as images flashed in his head of Maddie's fascination with the stallion. There wasn't a day that went by where he hadn't caught her communicating with the horse. She'd detour her way around the ranch just to make eye contact with him. And lately, he noticed the stash of sugar cubes in the pantry diminishing. Maddie hadn't fooled him. She took her coffee black, but she sure as hell had found another use for those sugar cubes.

Out of the darkness a black blur raced right past him. It was Storm. He snorted and dashed around the exterior perimeter of the corral. Five feet away from him, Storm halted. The stallion's black eyes bore into him as air pushed rapidly from his nostrils, a frenzied noise against the silence. He raised his front legs, balancing precariously and reared back in a desperate attempt to release the gear imposed upon him.

Trey took a hard swallow. His pulse beat like crazy.

Storm wore a *saddle*.

And his rider was missing.

Chapter Seven

Trey held Maddie in his arms, shielding her with his body from the dust swirling around in gusts. He'd been lucky to find her so quickly. His instincts hadn't failed him, and he was grateful his hunch had been right. He'd driven his truck like a demon through the dust storm, fearing the worst and praying for a miracle.

On the drive up here, Uncle Monty's words kept repeating in his head. "Don't lose that girl, boy."

Trey had never known such fear. The thought of losing Maddie had eaten away at him, corroding his insides. He didn't know if he'd find her in time. He didn't know the extent of her injuries. When he'd seen a saddled Storm with no rider, he'd immediately realized the dangers Maddie could have encountered. An unmerciful dust storm had moved through the territory. The stallion must have startled, throwing Maddie. Fortunately she'd landed on soft grass.

He gazed down at her slightly bruised face. She smiled and relief poured through him like a rushing river. He smiled back and another realization struck him hard, right between the eyes.

He had fallen for her.

If he'd doubted that at all an hour ago, he knew it for certain now. He'd never known he could feel so intensely, never known he could fall so hard.

"Maddie." He stroked her face, gently, careful not to touch the bruise on her cheek. She had a small gash across her forehead also but it had already stopped bleeding.

She looked up at him as if surprised. "Trey, you found me."

The wind continued to howl. Trey's shirt billowed, making flapping noises against his chest. "I've got to get you inside the truck," he said. "Can I lift you?"

"I'm s-sore," she said, "but I don't think anything's broken."

Trey relied on her good judgment as a doctor, relieved that she believed she hadn't broken a limb or cracked a rib. He hunkered down, using his body to block the wind and carefully lifted her. "Hang onto me."

Her arms wrapped around his neck and she clung on. "You okay?"

She nodded.

"I'll have you in the truck in no time," he assured her. Taking careful steps he strode to the passenger side of his truck, setting her gently onto the seat and then ran around to his side and climbed in. Quickly, he closed the door as wind blasts struck the truck, shaking it. "Don't worry. This old truck has weathered more than a fair share of these storms.

Mother Nature hasn't beaten her yet."

Maddie was tousled and roughed up a bit but apparently not injured and Trey's relief had him almost shaking along with the truck.

"Are you angry with me?" Her voice squeaked out.

Trey ran a hand through his hair and sighed. "More like scared spitless, honey. I didn't know what I'd find when I got up here."

Maddie closed her eyes. "I'm sorry."

Trey grabbed his first-aid kit from behind the seat and sidled up next to her. "I should be rightfully pissed, but I'm too doggone relieved right now. Hold still," he said, ripping open an antiseptic wipe and dabbing at the cut on her forehead then the bruise on her face.

She didn't flinch, taking her medicine like a good patient.

"What happened to Storm?"

"He's back at the ranch. I didn't stick around long enough to see to him, though."

"We were doing fine, really, Trey. He'd progressed so far, but it was his first time out with a rider and . . ."

"And he wasn't ready, Maddie. Don't make me think about that right now." Trey knew his anger would settle in later, after he got back to the ranch. Maddie had taken a stupid chance with Storm. She could have been killed or seriously injured. He might not have found her in time. But Trey shoved aside those worries for now, grateful that he *had* found her quickly and that she was safe. "I don't want to get riled up."

Maddie's green eyes rounded and she whispered softly, "You don't?"

Trey shook his head. "No," he said, spreading his legs out wide and gently reaching for her. "Come rest against me. Looks like we'll have to wait out the storm."

Maddie slid closer but it cost her to move. She'd be sore for days from that fall. Once she was snug against him, he wrapped his arms around her and rested her head just under his chin.

"Are you cold?"

Maddie shook her head.

"Scared?"

"Not anymore," she answered.

Trey angled his body so that he could slowly massage the muscles on her back. "How does this feel?"

Maddie crooned, "Better than a hot fudge sundae."

Trey smiled. "That good?"

Maddie nodded, laying her hand over his chest. If only she knew how fast his heart was beating at the moment. If only she knew how much holding and protecting her meant to him.

"Yeah, that good."

Furious blasts of wind continued to disturb the night, but they were safe and warm inside his truck and right now, that's all that mattered to Trey. With her body wedged against his, he could hold her all night long.

Maddie brought her head up, out of the crook of his arm to brush her sweet lips to his cheek. The kiss pumped his blood faster through his veins. "Thank you for coming to my rescue."

Trey brushed his hand through her hair as reddish waves spilled over his fingertips, soft and smooth and silky. "You nearly gave me a heart attack, Maddie," he whispered. "I'm gonna need a better thank-you."

Maddie slipped her hand inside an opened button on his shirt, stroking his flesh until his skin fairly sizzled. Then she lifted up and kissed him again, long and hard and beautifully Maddie.

"Was that better, Trey?"

"Better," he croaked, barely catching his breath.

Maddie stared into his eyes and every shred of willpower he could muster wasn't enough for the intoxicating look of desire she cast him. His manhood rose to the occasion, pressing against his jeans uncomfortably and Trey was at a complete loss, helpless to hold back. "Ah hell, Maddie," he whispered, brushing his lips to her ear, "how am I supposed to keep my hands off you now?"

A sweet triumphant smile emerged on her face. She spoke softly, "Maybe you're not supposed to, Trey. Maybe we were meant to be here together, trapped inside the truck, but trapped more by what our hearts are telling us."

"Yeah, maybe," Trey admitted, closing his eyes, allowing

her words to sink in. He ached for her physically, but his heart was involved too, and no matter how much he denied his feelings, he wanted Maddie with powerful, gut-wrenching need.

The storm raged outside. The truck trembled as wind gusts rocked them back and forth. Small particles of earth spiraled up to strike the windshield encasing them in darkness.

Trey *was* trapped by the storm, but he was also trapped by something stronger. His desire for Maddie. He knew if he touched her again, there would be no going back. Yet, he had to touch her. He had to feel her sleek skin under his palms, to slide his hands along her body and bring them both immeasurable pleasures. He'd fought the battle in his head long enough.

Trey stretched out, using the full "king" of the cab and pulled Maddie down with him, so that her petite frame lay across his. She fit him perfectly, the feel of her slight weight upon him an intoxicating elixir. He wove his fingers in her hair and claimed her lips, taking her in a slow, deliberate, there's-no-going-back-now kiss. Maddie moaned with pleasure and kissed him just as slowly, just as deliberately, moving on him to adjust her position and rubbing his body enough to destroy him.

He ached for her. He'd never been so turned on in his life. He'd never *wanted* so much. He kissed her forehead, her cheeks, her nose, then stroked his tongue over her mouth.

She opened for him and they kissed again, openmouthed and frenzied, with heat building and all semblance of grace disappearing. She was as hot for him as he was for her. He tore his mouth away long enough to whisper, "We have too many clothes on."

Without hesitation, Maddie sat up, pressing her derriere to his manhood, and unbuttoned her blouse. She took her time removing it. The ache below his waist grew harder with each second. Trey's body pulsed with need, and when she unhooked her soft white cotton bra and her breasts spilled out, he went hot all over. "You're beautiful, honey."

"Thank you." She smiled and leaned forward. "Now it's your turn," she said softly and began unbuttoning his shirt. Trey helped her. He couldn't get the damn thing off fast enough. And once done, he pulled her down again, crushing her breasts to his chest, molding her soft full flesh to his. Raw and powerful need assailed him. He took her in a wild, erotic kiss and then moved his mouth to her throat, kissing her, loving her, cupping her breasts in his hands, flicking his thumb over two erect pink peaks.

Maddie moaned.

Trey cursed, the need in him strong.

They were both lost.

He took her in his mouth then, his tongue stroking over one breast, moistening the rosy, pebbled nipple until Maddie sighed with pleasure. She wove her hand in his hair and guided him, showing him with each move, each little sound, what she enjoyed, what brought her satisfaction.

Trey wanted to please her. He wanted to bring her every ounce of enjoyment he possibly could. This was no one-night stand, where his mind wasn't attached to his body. He cared too much for Maddie not to make it good for her. And he wanted to make it damn good.

"Baby," she pleaded ever so softly.

One plea, one softly spoken word from Maddie turned him inside out.

Baby.

Trey's heart slammed against his chest. Powerful sensations ran a track race throughout his body. An overwhelming need to possess this woman, body and soul, struck him as hard as a staggering car crash. "Hold on, honey."

He reached down to unzip her jeans and slipped his hand inside, meeting with soft silk and lace. He played with the thin strap, amazed that this sensible, levelheaded doctor wore sexy panties.

"A thong?" he asked, hooking his finger under the strap.

She chuckled. "I'm afraid so."

"Damn." He was done for. He knew that from this moment on whenever he'd see her on the ranch wearing her clinical lab coat, an erotic image would instantly flash in his head. Maddie Brooks and her mind-blowing thong.

Trey kissed her again as he spread his hand flat against her belly and stroked her slowly. She whimpered, a little throaty sound that made his erection granite hard. He moved his fingers over her petal flesh, sliding back and forth, slowly, and erotically, bringing her pleasure and feeling her sweet heat. She rocked with him now, both lost in the rhythm as their bodies ground together in unison.

"I hope to God I have a condom," he muttered.

Maddie wove her fingers through his hair and gazed at him with half-lidded dewy eyes, her lips full and love-bruised, her sexy little body damp and slick. Trey no longer hoped; he prayed he had a rubber in his wallet.

She pressed her mouth against his chest, laving his nipples with her tongue until he ached so much he had to lift her off him. "Let's get naked."

Pants and boots were tossed off in a hurry. Trey fumbled around in his jeans, opened his wallet and pulled out a wrinkled foil packet. Instant relief washed over him. He didn't know what he'd have done otherwise.

Maddie took the packet from his hand and arched a brow. "Should I be glad you carry this around in your wallet?" she asked, and Trey understood she wasn't exactly teasing.

"It's old, Maddie. Ancient. This brand is nearly obsolete."

Maddie smiled and ripped open the packet. "Old is good, Trey."

"It's the truth."

Then she fitted the condom over his erection and lifted up, positioning herself over him. He slipped inside her, causing a little moan to escape her lips and sensation after sensation rocked him to the core. He'd never experienced anything so powerful in his life.

The storm had ended and a sliver of moonlight lit the cab, shining upon Maddie as she rode him up and down, her movements graceful and slow and as heady a sight as Trey had ever seen. Trey took the pleasure she offered, fascinated by the beautiful woman making love to him, stunned by the woman creating her own kind of storm.

Watching her face change with each stroke, each undulation with eyes closed and her head thrown back, Trey's heart raced, his body shook and his soul—she'd touched that as well. "You're amazing."

"Trey, I've never . . . " But she didn't finish her thought. She didn't have to. Trey knew. He felt the same way.

He guided her, helping her drive harder, faster, her breasts heaving, her hair flying as her body grew ready.

"Hold on, honey," he said, wanting to make this last as long as possible for reasons he couldn't deal with at the moment. For now, he wanted to prolong the night, prolong the pleasure.

Maddie's only response was a slight little encouraging sound.

Trey lifted her and together they rolled, bumping heads into the steering wheel and dashboard, until finally, she was under him. He kissed her again and again, touching her all over, breathing in the sexy scent of an aroused woman. Trey was more aroused than he'd ever been before.

Maddie rested her back against the window, held on to the steering wheel for support and Trey too grabbed the steering wheel, entering her with one thrust that shook him violently. "Ah, Maddie," he groaned, the pleasured pain almost too much to bear.

"Trey," she uttered.

Trey was lost. He moved like lightning, driving deep into her and watching her expression shift from pleasure to something more. She moved with him, rocking when he rocked, rising when he rose and trembling when he trembled.

He took her lips in one final deep kiss as he reached the highest plateau, taking her with him to a place he had never been before. With Maddie, everything seemed different, headier, sweeter. They combusted at the same time, Maddie's sighs and moans echoing in his ears. Together and slowly, they came down to Earth. His brain couldn't wrap around the sensations floating over his sated body. Too many emotions battled in his head.

She quivered and he held her tight as minutes ticked by in silence, both of them needing the time to face reality. He'd almost forgotten what she'd been through tonight. And he hoped like hell he hadn't hurt her. He maneuvered her so that she sat beside him. "Are you okay?"

Maddie nodded. "A bit overwhelmed. That was . . ."

"Incredible?"

She peered into his eyes as soft light glimmered into the cab. "More than that, Trey. It was much more than incredible."

Trey's breathing began to slow and his brain finally kicked into gear. A mounting uneasy tremor coursed through his body.

He'd given in to his desire.

He'd made love to Maddie.

Now, her pretty eyes filled with hope and expectation.

And Trey realized that he had done the thing he swore he would never do.

MADDIE SAT IN the passenger side of the truck in front of the ranch house, watching Trey shut down the engine. After they'd made love, they'd dressed quickly and quietly and rode home in silence, Trey's expression growing dimmer each second.

Maddie's emotions had been on a roller-coaster ride for much of the evening. First the fright of being tossed off Storm and left alone in bad weather; then the great relief that came when Trey rescued her. Confined in the truck and filled with strong desire, they'd made love. For Maddie, there weren't sufficient words to describe making love to Trey—a dream come true, her fantasy in the flesh. She'd ridden a high she'd never known, discovered sensations she never knew existed and now this—Trey's silent withdrawal, his distant body language.

"Trey?" she asked finally. He hadn't made a move to get out of the truck. He just sat there, running a hand down his face, seeming to do battle with something going on in his head. "I need to know where we go from here?"

Trey turned to face her, a look of deep regret and anguish crossing his features. The look alone frightened her, and she almost couldn't bear to hear what he had to say. But Maddie had never been a wilting willow—she fought her battles head on.

"That's just it, honey. There's nowhere to go from here."

Stunned, Maddie sat there for a moment, letting his words sink in. He couldn't possibly mean that it was over before it began. He couldn't possibly mean that tonight meant nothing to him. Nothing but . . . sex. Maddie tried not to spit the words out bitterly, "So that's it? A one-night stand?"

"No," he said adamantly. "You could never be a one-night stand."

"Then, what are you saying?" Maddie fought tears, barely keeping her emotions in check and waiting patiently for Trey's explanation.

Trey sighed deeply and peered out the truck's windshield. "I never meant for any of this to happen, Maddie. I tried keeping to our business agreement. Things got out of control."

Maddie held her chin high. "We made love and it was wonderful, Trey. But apparently, it didn't mean anything to you."

"It meant something to me," he rushed out. "That much is more than true."

"Just great sex?"

"The best sex of my life, Maddie. I won't deny that. But it was more."

Maddie closed her eyes. She believed him and should have been elated at Trey's admission but instead all she felt was gut-wrenching sorrow. She knew a brush-off when she heard one and feared what was coming next.

He scrubbed his jaw and took a deep breath. "I don't want to hurt you."

"Then don't."

His expression softened, his eyes brimming with regret. "I'm trying not to, Maddie. I'm trying damn hard to protect you."

"Protect me? From who? From . . . you?"

"Well, yeah."

Trey paused and Maddie waited.

"I'm no good with commitment," he said finally. "I've failed too many times in the past. I have a bad track record with women. And the trait goes back generations. It's like a curse."

"Trey, I don't recall asking you for a commitment."

Trey pushed air out of his lungs. "No way, Maddie. I

may not know a whole lot about women, but I do know one thing. You are definitely not a one-night, one-week or one-month stand. You're a keeper. You're the kind of woman that settles a man. I wish I was the settling kind, but I know I'm not. I don't commit. I've tried and failed. Did you know I was once engaged?"

His confession pinged straight to her heart. It hurt like hell picturing Trey involved with another woman. Offering her marriage. "No."

"Yeah, I was. And I left my fiancée just before the wedding. I ran off like a stupid fool and hurt her real bad. Left her to make all the explanations. Left her to deal with a broken heart. It really tore her up. I knew then that my fate was sealed. I'm just like my father and his father before him. They took what they wanted with no regard for the women who would get hurt. My father wasn't a bad man. He just didn't come to recognize his faults, until it was too late—five wives too late. The days of Will Walker are long gone. My great-great-grandfather was loyal. He had clarity. He knew what he wanted and went after it. He toughed it out and didn't give up. He had what I lack, Maddie. *Staying power.*"

Maddie's heart ached, yet she found herself wanting to know more. Maybe it was the healer in her, or maybe it was just morbid curiosity, but she wanted to learn about Trey's one-time engagement. "How long ago were you engaged?"

"I was twenty-one. Ten years ago, give or take."

"You were young, Trey. You weren't ready."

She thought about her good friend, Caroline, and what she'd been through because of a man who hadn't been ready. He'd abandoned his wife and child, yet Maddie had a hard time comparing the two men. Trey was too good a man to abandon his family, but it was clear that he believed he would, and right now, that's all that mattered—what Trey believed about himself.

"I was ready enough to ask her to marry me. I was ready enough to set a wedding date. I was ready enough to make plans for a future. Only thing I wasn't ready for was following through on my promises. Like I said, no staying power."

"And you think you'll break my heart?"

Trey closed his eyes briefly, "Yeah." A frustrated sigh spilled out of his mouth as he studied her. "I'll break your heart"

She threw caution and all good sense to the wind. "Maybe I'm willing to take that chance."

Trey shook his head. "I can't let you do that. You deserve better than me. You deserve someone who has everything to offer you. Someone steady."

"Like Nick Spencer?" Maddie didn't know exactly why she'd brought Nick's name up, but she had and now she wanted to see Trey's reaction. She and Nick were friends, period. But somehow she doubted Trey believed that, and a small part of her had rejoiced when she'd thought he'd been jealous of Nick.

Trey became quiet and long moments ticked by. Then

he finally nodded, "Yeah, if he makes you happy."

Maddie wanted to scream. Trey was the one who made her happy. He's the one she'd wanted since the day she stepped foot in Hope Wells. He's the one who had just made earth-shattering, mind-blowing, heart-stopping love to her.

She decided to lay it all on the line, to let him know the truth about Nick's proposal. If Trey cared for her at all, she'd find out right now. "Nick's part of a new clinic being developed in Denver, and he wants me to work alongside him there. The clinic will have all the latest state-of-the-art equipment, and we'd be on the ground floor of many new techniques in veterinary medicine. It would mean leaving my practice. It would mean saying goodbye to Hope Wells for good."

Trey's expression faltered for a moment, and she witnessed deep regret in his eyes. He spoke so quietly that Maddie had a hard time hearing him. "Maybe you should go."

A sharp slap in the face couldn't have stung more. Tonight, they'd shared something powerful, something special, something *beautiful*. They'd made love like their lives depended on it. And now, Trey dismissed her. Easily. Without much debate or thought. He'd simply decided what was best for her. He wouldn't even give them a chance. He didn't care enough to try.

The pain went deep. Tears threatened to spill, and she couldn't hold back any longer. She turned away from him and pulled the car door open. Climbing out of the truck, her feet hit the ground making swift strides to the porch. She took the steps quickly and opened the door to the house without bothering to look back.

Once inside, away from Trey's watchful eyes, her shoulders slumped and she let loose cries that tore from her throat. Hurrying down the hallway, she entered her bedroom and slammed the door. The jolt resounded against the walls and broke the desolate silence of the house. The big, comfy bed welcomed her, a cozy quilt and her pillow her only friends on such a lonely night. She flung herself down, grabbing her pillow to stifle her sobs.

The highs and lows of Trey's affection tonight knifed through her so sharply she didn't know if she would ever heal. But she had some pride left. Enough that she didn't want Trey to walk into the house and hear her crying.

She reached for a tissue on the nightstand and dabbed her eyes, blew her nose. Her breathing steadied. A false sense of calm settled her. For now, she would be fine. For now, she would accept Trey's decision. What choice did she have? He couldn't have been any clearer.

He believed he had no staying power.

Maddie walked over to the window and peered out into the night. A shadow of a figure emerged through the darkness. It was Trey. He pulled a lead rope with Storm on the other end. The stallion kicked up a fuss, but Trey held firm and instead of retiring the stallion in his corral, he led him to the stables. He'd most likely stay up the rest of the night settling the horse, making sure he was calm.

Maddie had always thought Trey was so like Storm. Two wild spirits, two untamed souls who didn't know how to trust. She'd been with both tonight, optimistically thinking the two had been ready and hoping the bond she'd developed with each had been enough. Maddie had tested the waters and had nearly drowned. And she'd come to realize one distinct difference between Storm and his master. While Storm couldn't trust in others, Trey couldn't trust in himself.

But Maddie saw Trey so differently than he saw himself.

He claimed he couldn't commit, but Maddie knew better. She knew him to be a man of worth, and if she decided to leave the ranch, Hope Wells, and Trey Walker behind, she'd try to help him learn the truth about himself before she left.

She figured she didn't have anything to lose.

Her heart was already broken.

DAWN FORCED ITS way through dark clouds, shedding dismal light and bringing a frosty chill to the air. Maddie showered quickly and dressed in her usual attire, jeans and a button-down blouse, then quickly headed to the barn where Storm was stabled. She had to make amends with the stallion. She'd pushed him too far last night and even though he'd responded to her more than any other person on the ranch, they still had a long way to go.

She wrapped her arms around her middle and entered the damp barn, realizing that while Trey had the means to heat the barn for the animals, he didn't have the funds. Only extreme temperatures warranted going to that expense.

Her friend, Caroline had joked about the unpredictable weather conditions in this part of Texas, and she wasn't too far off the mark. "If you don't like the weather in Texas, just wait about five minutes," she'd said.

This week had gone from warm sunny days to gusty dust storms and cold temperatures. She wondered about Denver and how well she would adjust to the climate there. In truth, she'd stayed up most of the night considering Nick's proposal, thinking about moving and wondering if leaving Hope Wells might be best for her.

Maddie put that thought out of her head as she walked up to Storm's stall. The horse rested on his side on a bed of wheat straw that was piled up high around the edges. With Storm's restless nature, a good bank of bedding against the walls insured the animal's safety. Trey always put his animals first whenever he could. It was probably the first trait that had attracted Maddie to him—his willingness to protect his livestock.

"Morning."

Maddie whirled around and stared into the dark eyes of a

rumpled Trey. His appearance, including an unshaven face and disheveled hair, reminded her that if things had turned out differently last night, she would have been waking up to that look today.

"He's all right." He gestured to Storm. "Took some time to get him settled, but we managed."

Maddie nodded. "You stayed with him all night?"

"Most of it. Didn't get much sleep."

Trey scratched his head and then ran a hand through his hair. The attempt to straighten the unruly strands only made them stick up even more. His plaid shirt hung loosely over jeans that were smattered with dirt stains and sticky straw. Maddie wondered how a man could appear incredibly vulnerable and downright sexy all at the same time.

She ached inside, seeing him and knowing that what they shared would never be again. Maddie struggled against the pain, determined to keep her composure.

"Actually, I'm glad you're here," he said quietly. She wondered if he ached inside the way that she did. "I was planning on checking on you. How are you feeling this morning?"

Did he want to know her heart had broken?

"You took a fall and . . . well after, when we—"

"I'm fine, Trey." She couldn't bear to discuss their lovemaking from last night. She couldn't speak to him casually about something that had meant so much to her. He'd made his feelings known, rejecting even the thought of a relationship with her. Yes, she'd been terribly hurt, but not from the fall.

Trey swallowed and looked away.

Maddie turned to leave. It seemed there wasn't much else to say. She came to check on Storm, and the poor animal looked exhausted. Apparently it had been a tumultuous night for all three of them. She promised herself to return later to make amends with the stallion.

"Maddie?"

She turned around. "Yes?"

Trey's gaze held her immobile. "You might not believe this, but I don't regret last night."

She did believe him. Didn't he say he'd never had better sex? At least she had that to cling to on lonely nights. "Neither do I," she replied honestly.

She walked to the barn door and then turned once again to find Trey's dark captivating eyes on her. "You know, it was a lucky day for Storm when you brought him to 2 Hope. You've stuck by him all along, believing in that feisty, headstrong stallion, even when others gave up on him. There aren't too many men who would have spent half the night in a cold, dreary barn worrying over him. He *does* belong to you, Trey. Just like you belong to him."

Trey's brows rose in surprise, and his thoughtful expression left Maddie with a gladdened heart. She walked away with a smile.

Chapter Eight

UNDER ORDINARY CIRCUMSTANCES, Maddie would have looked forward to an evening with new friends. But tonight, her heart simply wasn't up for it. She stared in her bedroom mirror to find a woeful reflection looking back. Her bleak mood matched the gloomy rain they'd been experiencing for days now. How was she going to pull herself together enough to share a dinner with Trey and his friends Paul and Brittany tonight?

She held up the lovely, handwritten invitation and reread the beginning sentiment. *The pleasure of your company is requested.* Maddie had almost forgotten all about this invitation until Brittany called yesterday specifically making sure Maddie would come. She'd been caught off guard and fumbled around in her head for an excuse, but Brittany's sweet demeanor and hopeful tone made her change her mind. She didn't want to disappoint the woman and Maddie had to face facts. She couldn't hide from Trey Walker. They lived in the same house.

She'd treaded carefully, trying not to purposely bump into him these past few days. That hadn't been too difficult a task, since she'd been working long hours, taking on appointments, going out on house calls, and making referrals when her limited ability to treat the animals hadn't been enough. After the night when she'd taken off on Storm, she'd been swamped with work. She welcomed the distraction.

Trey hadn't been around the house much either. She'd see him on cloudy mornings ride off on his horse with Kit or some of the other ranch hands, doing what cowboys do, but she didn't look for him at night. She'd retire to her bedroom in the evening with a good book, trying to put thoughts of him out of her head.

With a deep sigh, Maddie fingered the silver necklace around her neck. "I've got a big decision to make, Aphrodite." Nick's proposal was never far from her mind. He'd given her some much-needed time to make her decision, but she knew he couldn't wait indefinitely. He had a time frame and Maddie wouldn't take advantage of his good nature. She'd have to come to her decision soon.

From down the hall, she could hear the shower door open and close, and water pelting down, reminding her that Trey also readied for the dinner party tonight. And as she moved about her room, shedding her work clothes, she heard his sounds. She'd become familiar with the noises he made while getting dressed.

Maddie donned a pair of tan slacks and a soft buttercream scoop-neck sweater. She dressed her outfit up with drop pearl earrings and a matching bracelet. She debated whether to wear the pearl necklace that matched the set, but she didn't have the heart to remove Aphrodite. If ever she needed to feel a bond, that special closeness to Grandma Mae, it was now. Okay, so she wouldn't make the greatest fashion statement tonight, but she'd have something more important.

Maddie styled her hair, letting the stubborn waves fall where they may, and gave it a quick spray. She grabbed her purse, took one last look in the mirror, and pasted on a smile. The transition was complete. She was ready for the evening. With a yank, she opened the door and batted her eyes. Trey stood at the threshold, his hand fisted as if he were about to knock.

"Trey?" She took a step back and stared. He looked better than sin itself in dark trousers, a white dress shirt, and a thin black bolo tie decorated with a triangle of turquoise. His hair, pushed back from his face and still a little damp, exposed clean-shaven skin, high cheekbones, and unreadable dark eyes. "Are you almost ready?" he asked.

Maddie swallowed. "Uh, ready?"

He nodded. "For dinner at Paul and Brit's?"

She'd never seen Trey in anything but jeans and a work shirt. The man cleaned up nicely. Suddenly Maddie felt underdressed for the occasion. "Yes, but I think I need to change. Maybe I should wear a dress," she mumbled.

She made a move to shut her door. Trey put up his hand

to hold the door ajar, halting her from retreating into her room. "You look beautiful, Maddie."

"But, I—"

He offered again, more firmly, "Look. Beautiful."

Her heart did a little flip. It wasn't often Trey offered up a compliment. Yet, Maddie thought that he was the one who looked beautiful, and she wondered if she'd be able to keep from staring at him all night.

Maddie gave him a smile. "Thank you. I guess I'll see you over there." She brushed by him, catching a delectable whiff of lime and musk aftershave. The whole Trey package was hard for her to ignore. It wasn't fair. He was definitively the most appealing man on Earth.

"I figured we'd go together."

Maddie stopped in the hallway. "Why would you figure that?"

"Because the rain's only going to get worse. A T-storm is brewing and the roads might get washed out. It only makes sense, we're going to the same place, and we'll be returning back here when it's over."

Maddie knew she was being unreasonable, but she didn't want to arrive at the dinner party with Trey. She didn't want to be drawn to him anymore than she already was. She didn't want to sit next to him in the truck and be reminded of the night they'd made love. She couldn't face any of those things right now. She spoke softly and directly into his eyes. "I think it's best if we go separately, Trey."

Trey stood firm, pursed his lips in displeasure then inhaled deeply. "If that's what you want."

None of this was what Maddie wanted. But Trey hadn't given her much of an option to her wants and desires. He hadn't given them a chance, but that wouldn't stop her from making him see his own potential. If she could leave him with one gift, it would be to make him trust in himself again.

Even though she'd been hurt, she wasn't angry at Trey any longer. She understood him, and where he believed he had a weakness, she saw only a loss of faith. Once his faith was restored, Trey Walker could move on with his life.

She gave him a slow nod then walked to the kitchen. Opening the refrigerator, she removed a frosted lemon layer cake and carefully set it onto a large plate.

Trey followed her and stood in the doorway. "What's that?"

"I baked a lemon cake this afternoon."

"You . . . baked?"

Maddie chuckled. "For what it's worth, I did."

"Lemon's my favorite."

Maddie glanced at Trey's puzzled expression. She'd learned a lot about Trey Walker lately, but she hadn't known his favorite . . . anything. "It was Brittany's suggestion."

"Oh."

"She and Paul think the world of you, Trey. You've been a good friend to them, working at their place nonstop, and even after you hurt your hand—"

"Hell, it was a scratch, Maddie."

"And even after that, you went back to finish the job you'd started. That new baby is going to have a wonderful nursery, thanks to you. Your friends want to show their appreciation."

Trey found the floor real interesting then, scratching the back of his head. "They don't have to do this."

"They *want* to. I imagine there'll be a lot of your favorites at dinner tonight."

Trey stepped closer to stare into her eyes. He tucked a finger under her chin and cast her a heart-melting smile. "I imagine so."

"Trey?" The blood in her veins warmed.

"You're one of my favorites, Maddie," he whispered and bent his head.

Maddie couldn't allow him to kiss her. She'd fall deeper and harder than ever, and that would prove disastrous. She retreated, whispering, "Cross me off your list."

Trey's head popped up. He ran a hand down his jaw, staring at her lips with regret in his eyes. "I'm trying," he said solemnly, as if caring for her was the worst of all possible options. And sadly, Maddie knew that in his heart Trey really believed his loving her would be her downfall. "Trouble is, I'm crazy about you."

Maddie wanted to shout the famous movie line, "*Snap out of it.*" But instead, she grabbed the cake plate and headed to the front door, muttering under her breath, "Maybe, we're both just plain crazy."

A LITTLE BIT of hurt was far better than a whole world of hurt, Trey rationalized, as he sat on a wing chair in the Fuller parlor, sipping beer. Trey knew that he'd hurt Maddie the other night. He hadn't meant to. He hadn't meant to touch her, much less make love to her. But he'd come to his senses far too late and even now he didn't regret that night. How could he, when everything had been so perfect? How could he regret the best night of his life?

He couldn't be sorrier about rejecting Maddie, but it had been his only option because she deserved more. She deserved a fair chance in life. She deserved a man who would be there through thick or thin, a man who could weather any of life's storms, a man with staying power.

Trey would never forget the sober, nearly desperate look on his father's face, when he'd spoken those last bitter, haunting words. "Don't make the same mistakes I made, son." Trey hadn't told a soul, but today was the anniversary of his father's death. And today, more than ever, his father's plea had stuck in his mind with dawning clarity.

Then he'd gone and witnessed Maddie lifting a two-layer cake from the refrigerator with pride in her eyes. He liked the idea of Maddie Brooks baking his favorite cake for him. He'd lost all sense of clarity then and tried to kiss her.

Stupid move.

She'd been right to step away. She'd been right to protect her heart. Trey had little willpower when it came to Maddie. But he wouldn't subject her to that whole world of hurt. Hooking up with Trey Walker meant disaster to any decent woman and she was the last person he wanted to injure.

Outside, the storm raged. Thunder boomed and lightning illuminated the night's sky, yet all seemed peaceful inside the parlor with licking flames crackling in the fireplace. Maddie sat on the sofa next to Paul and Jack. She'd been introduced to a few others as well, and everyone held a tall glass of champagne in their hands. Everyone except Trey and Jack. Walker men didn't drink anything with bubbles.

"It's time for a toast," Paul said, standing and holding up his glass. Brittany stood beside him, her glass filled with sparkling cider. All the others stood as well. "To Trey," Paul began, "our good friend. We couldn't have finished the baby's room without you. You worked hard, my friend," Paul said sincerely, then winked, "and even after we tried to kill you with that wood beam, you came back to finish the job. That's friendship."

"Or stupidity," Jack interjected and everyone chuckled.

Brittany slugged him in the arm. Then she moved into the forefront and spoke softly. "And if we have a boy," she said, darting a quick, loving glance at Paul, "we've decided that Trey would make a fine middle name for our son."

Overcome by Paul and Brittany's kind gesture, Trey

stood speechless, glancing at his friends.

"To Trey Walker," Paul repeated, clinking his glass to Trey's beer bottle first.

"Thank you," Trey said, surprised at the lump in his throat. He had trouble getting the words out. "I'm honored."

He glanced at Maddie. Her eyes had been on him, watching him, those pretty grass green sparks touching him, conveying her innermost thoughts. She fought it but he saw through her brave front of denial. She didn't hide her emotions well. In her eyes, he saw too many things. Hope. Expectation. Regret. Pain.

"It's time for dinner," Brittany announced. "Please everyone, come join us in the dining room."

Trey waited for the others to file out of the parlor. The scent of raspberries wafted right under his nose. Maddie was close by and as he turned, he found her next to him.

She reached up on tiptoes to whisper in his ear, "No staying power? You're a loyal friend, Trey. You wouldn't let your friends down. Paul and Brittany are naming their baby after you. They adore you, and I can understand why."

Before Trey could respond, Maddie sashayed away and left him standing there amid her sweet scent as she walked into the dining room.

It was hard to remember what his life had been like before she moved onto the ranch. And it'd be even more difficult imagining her gone. But Trey was certain she would leave Hope Wells now.

He'd messed up pretty badly, hurting her in the process. As much as he'd vowed not to get involved with her, proving her wrong would go a long way in protecting her. It was one thing to help out a friend, but committing his life to a woman was quite another. Trey feared he couldn't do it, and where would that leave Maddie?

He walked into the dining room with newfound determination. No matter how much pain her leaving would cause him, he knew he'd have to suffer it out. He and Maddie had no future together at 2 Hope Ranch.

"YOU'RE IN LOVE with her, Trey," Brittany said, wiping her hands on a dish towel in the kitchen.

"With who?" Trey glanced around the deserted kitchen. Hell, he'd only come in here to thank Brit privately for the wonderful meal. She'd made all of his favorite things: chicken croquettes, sweet potato pie, creamed corn, and fresh baked biscuits.

Brit cast him an irritated look. He knew she wasn't going to give up until they had this conversation.

"With Maddie, and don't get cute."

"Me? I've never been accused of being cute."

"That's because you're drop-dead handsome, Trey. It seems as though Maddie thinks so, too. You two couldn't keep your eyes off each other tonight."

Trey shrugged.

"So are you or aren't you?"

Trey shut his eyes briefly and inhaled. "Nope. I can't be."

Brit leaned against the back of the counter, her belly protruding out and round as a beach ball. She looked lovely pregnant. And when she placed a protective hand on her abdomen, rubbing slightly, Trey wondered what it would be like fathering a child of his own. Maddie's image instantly appeared in his mind. With no barriers to his thoughts, he saw her carrying his baby, resting her hand over her swollen belly and giving him a loving smile.

"You *can't* be? What's that supposed to mean?"

"It means, I wouldn't do that to her."

Brit chuckled. "I think she'd want you to do that to her. Over and over again."

"Brit!"

"Well, I didn't get pregnant all by myself, Trey. I'm not that innocent. And I can see there's something strong between you. Are you denying it? And remember, Paul and I are your closest friends, so no fair fibbing."

Trey let out a deep sigh. "No, I'm not denying it. There's definitely something there. Maddie's pretty darn wonderful."

Brit reached for his hand, flipping it over to view his injured palm. "So are you, Trey. You deserve some happiness in your life. You've been alone too long."

Trey squeezed her hand and smiled. "At least this way, no one gets hurt."

"Or maybe both of you get hurt."

Jack busted into their conversation striding into the kitchen at full speed. He spoke quiet enough so the guests in the dining room wouldn't hear, but as forcefully as Trey had ever heard him. "Are you nuts or something?"

Trey shook his head. He seemed to be on the receiving end of one of his cousin's tirades. "What now, Jack?"

"Maddie told us that she's thinking of leaving Hope Wells. She's been offered a job in Denver."

"She has?" Brit pointed a look at him.

"Yeah, I know."

"And you're not going to stop her?" Jack asked.

"It's her decision."

"Shit." Jack caught himself with a shake of his head. "Sorry, Brit. But hell, Trey's being a jerk."

"You could ask her not to go," Brit said sweetly.

"Hell yeah. Give that girl a reason to stay, Trey," Jack added.

Trey hated being backed into a corner. He'd already made his decision regarding Maddie and was trying damn hard to abide by it. What right did anyone have to judge him? Anger simmered close to his breaking point. He stepped away from his cousin to avoid coming to blows. "Jeez, if you're so damn interested, maybe you should ask her to stay."

"Maybe I will."

Trey ground out, "Good."

"Great. I backed off before because of you, but I like her a lot. What's not to like? She's smart and funny and pretty as a picture. Hell, if you're too much of a fool to see it, then I'm going to ask her out."

Trey grabbed Jack's shirt and pulled him so they stood nose to nose. "You don't want to go there, cousin. Or you might have to arrest me for assaulting an officer."

Jack grinned and craned his neck to look at Brit. "He's in love with her."

Brit agreed. "You're in love with her."

Trey released Jack and they backed away from each other. He glanced at Brit then back to Jack. Both wore smug expressions. "Damn meddlers. That's what you are."

"Are you calm now?" Jack asked.

Trey twisted his lips. "Ticked off, but calm."

Maddie walked in with Paul right behind her carrying dishes from the dining room. "Thought I could help you in here, Brittany." Maddie set the dishes down on the counter by the sink.

"Oh, isn't that sweet."

"Looks like you've got plenty of help already. What're you boys doing taking up with an ole pregnant lady?" Paul asked.

Brittany swatted him with the dish towel then glanced at Maddie. "You know, I think I'll wait up a bit on doing the dishes. These boys need some of your lemon cake to settle them down."

Maddie glanced around the room taking in their guilty expressions. "I hope it came out okay."

Brittany smiled. "I'm sure it's just fine. Trey'll think so, no matter what."

"I know, but my lemon cake might not be—"

"It'll be delicious, Maddie," Trey offered honestly.

"Because you baked it special for him," Brittany said with wink.

"Hey Maddie," Jack said, darting a quick glance at Trey, "you ever treat a stubborn old mule?"

"Well, yes I have." Her brows furrowed curiously. "I've had some experience with stubborn mules. Why?"

Jack grinned again, and Trey was about ready to slap that silly expression off his face. He shrugged. "I heard there's this mule in Hope Wells sorely in need of your attention."

Brittany chuckled, grabbed Maddie's hand and guided her out of the kitchen. "Come on, we'll let those boys bring in the dessert. It'll give them something constructive to do."

Paul stepped between Trey and Jack, heading off trouble.

"Paul," Trey said through pursed lips. "Next time you have a party for me, I'd appreciate it if you didn't invite my cousin."

Jack picked up the lemon cake, and laughed his way into the dining room.

MADDIE SAT BETWEEN Paul and a nice man named Burton, one of the Fuller's neighbors. She faced Trey and Brittany. Jack sat at the head of the table, placed there specifically by the hostess. Maddie got the feeling Jack's new seating arrangement wasn't so much by choice. Whatever Jack had been up to seemed to put a spur in Trey's hide. He'd been giving his cousin sour looks since they'd sat down. Jack didn't seem any worse for wear, he kept a smile on his face and every once in a while, she caught him watching her.

Paul poured coffee into delicate antique cups as Brittany reached over to cut the cake. She made a face and arched her back in a stretch that seemed to take some discomfort away. It wasn't the first time Maddie caught Brit looking uncomfortable. As a doctor, Maddie knew the female body was tested to its limit during gestation and maybe Brit had taken on too much with this celebration.

"It's so beautiful," Brittany said, gazing upon the lemon frosting swirls Maddie had designed with care. "I almost hate to cut into it."

"Then let me," Maddie offered. "I'd love to help out and serve the cake."

Brittany handed over the knife and cake server. "Be my guest." She plopped down into her seat, sighing deeply.

Maddie cut several slices and was just finishing sending the plates around the table when her cell phone rang. "Uh, sorry about that," she said to Brittany and Paul, "but I have to get this."

"No problem. We'll wait for you," Paul said.

She exited the room quickly and answered her phone.

One minute later she stood at the dining room threshold making apologies. "I'm sorry, but I have an emergency call. I have to leave."

"Oh, no. I'm sorry to hear that," Brittany said. "Is it urgent?"

"I'm afraid so. Darla Chester's dog is having a difficult birth. It's her first litter and Darla's beside herself with worry. I promised I'd come over right away."

Paul looked doubtful. "That's clear across the county, Maddie."

"And the storm's not letting up," Burton's wife, Tilly, announced as she looked out the window.

Jack volunteered, "I don't live far from there, I'd be happy to take—"

"I'll drive you." Trey pushed out his chair and stood.

Maddie glanced at the roomful of worried guests. "Oh, thank you all for your concern, but I'll be fine, really. I don't want to break up the party."

She felt really badly about this. Paul and Brittany had gone to a great deal of trouble tonight and Maddie hated being the one to spoil the rest of the evening. She'd learned early on in her profession that when duty calls, all else had to be forfeited. She didn't mind when her own plans were ruined, but she hated when it overflowed to others' lives.

"I'm driving you, Maddie." Trey announced.

"But you haven't taken a bite of your cake yet."

"I'll wrap up both of your pieces and send them along with you," Brittany offered, then added, "That's one nasty storm out there. I'd feel better knowing Trey was with you."

"So would I," Paul agreed, glancing out the window.

Brittany rose quickly taking both of their plates into the kitchen, while Trey strode over to her. "Do you have everything you need in your truck?"

"Yes, I keep it supplied in case of emergencies. But Trey, you really don't have to do this." Maddie glanced at the table of friends he would be leaving behind. "I'll manage. It's what I do."

"Honey," Trey whispered for her ears only, turning on the Walker charm, "if you don't let me drive you, I'm going to follow behind you all the way. You need to get there safely, and I know exactly where Darla lives."

Maddie had a hard time resisting Trey's offer, not because she feared the thunder that boomed like a demon's wail or the heavy rain teeming down, but because Trey spoke so sweetly, his dark, gorgeous eyes troubled and concerned.

Her heart ached knowing that Trey cared for her, but wouldn't act upon his feelings. He wouldn't break down the wall that kept them from being together. But Maddie couldn't think about that right now. She had puppies to deliver, and now it appeared she had a chauffeur to deliver her to the laboring Labrador. "Thank you," she said. "We'd better get going."

Brittany handed Trey a small brown bag. "I wrapped your cake inside." She reached up and kissed Trey on the cheek. "You're a wonderful friend, Trey. And our baby says thank you, too."

Trey leaned over to hug Brittany then shook Paul's hand. "You're welcome and dinner was great."

Trey said farewell to the others at the table and Maddie said her quick goodbyes as well, giving Brittany her special thanks for the evening.

"You two take it slow and easy now," Paul said, walking them to the front door. "And remember that Cody's Pass will be washed out by now."

Trey nodded. "I plan on avoiding the Pass. Don't worry. We'll get there just fine."

Paul opened the door and wind howled fiercely as cold air immediately chilled the warm room. A shiver ran down Maddie's spine. She hadn't seen weather like this in a decade or more.

"Hand me your keys, Maddie."

Maddie had no problem giving up her keys to Trey.

"You ready?" he asked, taking her hand and squeezing gently.

She nodded, hanging on to Trey's strong hand and they dashed outside.

Chapter Nine

AFTER A SLOW, laborious drive across the county, Trey delivered Maddie safely to the Chester house. Trey was steps behind her as she dashed inside dripping wet. To Maddie's chagrin, Darla greeted Trey affectionately. "Trey? I didn't expect to see you here. It's been a long time."

Trey's charming smile emerged as his gaze swept over Darla. "Hi, Darla. It has been a while. Maddie's not used to our T-storms, so I drove her here."

Darla gave her a glance, finally making the connection. "That's right, you're practicing out of 2 Hope now, Dr. Brooks."

"Yes. Temporarily." Maddie smiled, while her heart took a tumble. She'd never felt less a woman than now, soaked through her clothes with her hair plastered to her head. She'd bet her last dollar that her makeup was smudged beyond repair, while Darla Chester stood tall and graceful with long waves of blond hair falling nearly to her buttocks. Her thin frame only accentuated what Maddie would term a perfect namesake, Chester. The woman was extremely well endowed.

Funny, but Maddie had met Darla a few times when she'd treated her Lab at her office in town, but she hadn't felt any pangs of envy then. Now, she viewed Darla Chester in a whole new light—through Trey's eyes.

"I'm so darn worried about Candy. Thanks for coming out in this weather," Darla said, leading them into the kitchen. The yellow Labrador lay in her whelping box in the far corner, breathing heavily, trying as she might to deliver her pups.

Maddie instantly forgot about her insecurities and got to work. "She's so tired already." She massaged the dog, stroking her gently, rubbing her belly. "She's probably got five or six in there." Maddie glanced up at Trey. "This might take a while."

Trey bent down next to her, smelling like fresh rain and looking sexy as sin soaked through his clothes. Maddie didn't know how Trey Walker did it, but she'd never met a more appealing man in her life. "I'm staying for however long it takes, Maddie."

"Thanks."

"Put me to work," he said.

"Me, too, what can I do?" Darla asked, her amber eyes filled with concern.

"Well, first we have to get her up and moving. Normally I'd let her outside to stimulate her, but the weather's not cooperating. Does Candy have any favorite toys or anything she likes that might spark her interest?"

"Yes, she does," Darla answered.

"Good, because we're going to have to keep her busy."

They spent the next twenty minutes taking turns playing with the dog, trying to keep her mind off her tired uterus and stimulate her enough to allow nature to take its course. When Maddie thought she was ready, she guided her back down into her whelping box and the first pup eased out of her at half past midnight.

"That's a good girl, Candy," Maddie said, stroking her head gently.

The pup found her mama's teat easily and began suckling.

"Cute little thing," Trey said, his expression childlike, full of winsome interest. His reaction made her wonder how Trey would react to fatherhood. Though he would probably disagree, Maddie was certain Trey would make a terrific father. He had all the qualities necessary—patience, kindness, and a distinct affection for all beings, great and small.

"There's at least four more cuties like this in there," Maddie said, "but poor Candy's going to have to work hard through the night."

Darla walked up. "You folks must be cold and exhausted. I turned up the heat and made a pot of coffee. Forgive me. I should have offered it to you when you first arrived, but—"

"You were worried about Candy. That's only natural," Maddie responded.

Darla waved her over. "Come to the table. We can keep

our eyes on Candy from here."

Maddie glanced at the laboring Labrador and shook her head. "I think I'll stay by her side for now. She's a little unsure of things. You and Trey take a break. I'll be there in a few minutes."

"Are you sure?" Darla asked, biting her lip. "Is everything okay with her?"

"Everything's fine, really. It's just a precaution. Go on, you two and don't worry about us. We'll be fine."

Darla turned to Trey. "Coffee?"

"I'd love a cup."

"Cream, no sugar, right?" Darla asked.

Trey nodded. "You have a good memory."

Darla chuckled as they walked over to the table. "Sometimes I wish it wasn't so good."

Maddie concentrated on Candy, stroking her head and massaging her abdomen, but every once in a while she'd catch a bit of Darla and Trey's conversation. They'd laugh over something, then whisper softly. Maddie presumed by the way they spoke to each other that they'd known each other a long time, but she also got the impression something more had gone on between the two of them.

She told herself it was none of her business, but a niggling thought had stuck in her mind. Had Trey insisted he bring her here tonight so that he could see Darla? She glanced up just in time to witness Darla lay her hand on Trey's cheek. She couldn't hear their words, but their soft, quiet tone spoke volumes.

Candy made a whimpering noise and Maddie directed her attention back to the laboring dog. A minute later, the second pup was delivered.

"Hey, this one's a little bigger." Trey bent down and handed Maddie a cup of steaming hot coffee. "Here you go. I figured you could use this right about now."

Maddie leaned back against tile wall, now that she was sure Candy and the pups were all right, and sipped the coffee, "Mmmm, this is good."

"Hits the spot, doesn't it?" Trey smiled.

"Yeah, it does."

"You know, just in case I haven't told you this before, you're darn good at what you do."

She smiled. If there was one thing in her life that she could take pride in, it was her profession. She loved being a veterinarian. She couldn't think of a time when she wouldn't be working with animals. "Thanks."

Trey nodded and studied her face. "Why don't you get up for a while, stretch out. I'll watch Candy for a few minutes. Besides, I think Darla needs some encouragement. She's acting like a worried mother hen over there, but she doesn't want to get in your way."

"She really adores this dog."

Trey slid a quick glance Darla's way. "She's got a good heart."

Maddie spoke ever so quietly, the whisper barely audible.

"And did you break it, Trey?"

Trey looked into Maddie's eyes, hesitating with his answer. When he finally responded, his reply wasn't what she'd expected. "For years, I thought I had but that doesn't seem to be the case after all."

This wasn't the time or place to discuss his past loves, although Maddie couldn't deny that Trey's comment intrigued the heck out of her. Maddie rose and stretched, working the kinks out of her back and then walked over to Darla to reassure her that Candy was doing fine. She still had three or four more puppies to deliver.

If all went well, they'd be back at 2 Hope Ranch before sunup.

TREY STOMPED DIRT off his boots, hung up his hat on a peg by the back door and entered the kitchen. Maddie stood waiting for him by the kitchen table, fidgeting with a linen napkin she was about to set down. She'd been halfway through cooking this meal when she began to have second thoughts. Maybe Trey didn't like surprises. Maybe all he wanted to do was fall into bed after a hard day's work.

But Maddie owed him. He hadn't gotten a wink of sleep last night. It had been nearly dawn when they'd finally retired to their bedrooms this morning and just two hours later, Maddie heard Trey get up. She'd looked out the window to find Trey riding out into the rain-soaked, dreary morning.

Even though he'd insisted on driving her to Darla's house, Maddie still felt a pang of guilt at keeping him up all night. Exhausted and beat, she'd thanked him again when they'd arrived home, but it hadn't been enough. And while her culinary talents weren't top-notch, Maddie knew how to make killer tamales and Spanish rice, a Texas staple and something she'd learned from her friend, Caroline. Maddie had called her three times this afternoon, double-checking the recipe, making sure she hadn't forgotten anything.

"Hi." Maddie greeted Trey with trepidation and a big smile.

Trey glanced at the table she'd set with a pretty blue lace tablecloth she'd found in the linen closet along with mismatched napkins. Two tall tapered candles cast the room in mellow soothing light. "What's this?"

"Dinner and thank-you."

He lifted his nose in the air. "Smells delicious."

"Tamales and rice. Are you hungry?"

Trey grinned. "Is that a trick question?"

Maddie stumbled with her words. "Uh, well, I wasn't sure if you'd want to get right to bed, or, uh—"

Trey's eyes went wide, then a playful smile emerged. "That's the best offer I've had all day."

Maddie tossed the napkin at him, but he caught it before it struck his grinning face.

"It's an offer for *dinner,* you dopey cowboy."

With a teasing light still in his eyes, Trey admitted, "I know, but a man can dream, can't he?"

Maddie shook her head, ignoring his teasing comment, because she knew there was no real substance there. She knew Trey wasn't dreaming about her in or out of bed. "Dinner will be ready in ten minutes."

Trey walked up to her, coming extremely close and looked into her eyes. "You look real pretty tonight, Maddie."

Maddie blushed. She'd purposely dressed up, wanting to erase the horrible drowned-rat image from last night, when she'd gotten caught in the thunderstorm. Tonight, she wore a simple black dress, nothing too fancy, but a dress that made her feel womanly. "Thank you."

"Seems you're forever thanking me."

He slid the napkin back into her palm, and the slight brush of his hand was enough to warm her up all over. Then she stared deeply at him, really looking beyond his handsome features, noting that he didn't look tired at all. How can a man work and work and work, and not look like something the cat dragged in? "I thought you'd be exhausted by now. I felt bad all day, knowing you didn't get any sleep because of me."

"I slept."

"Yes, for about an hour early this morning."

Trey brushed his mouth to her ear, creating tingles Maddie struggled to conceal—tingles that made her knees go weak. He whispered his secret. "I slept today. Found me a nice dry patch of pasture and took a little nap. Didn't think I'd be able to keep my eyes open the rest of the day, otherwise."

"Oh."

Trey stepped back to gaze into her eyes. "Did you think I was Superman or something?"

"Maybe *or something*," she admitted.

The twinkle in his eyes, the smile on his lips did something wonderful to her. She'd never known anyone like Trey Walker before. She'd fallen in love with him almost from the first moment she'd met him, but she realized now, that she really hadn't loved Trey back then. She'd been fascinated by him and attracted by the gentle way he had with his animals. She'd been captivated by his good looks and intrigued by his polite yet distant demeanor. No, she hadn't loved him then, she knew that for fact.

Because she loved him now.

So much . . . so unnervingly much that she ached deep in her heart. This love was real. This love was pure. It struck her like a knife, sharp and swift.

She had come to know the real Trey Walker and had fallen head over heels.

Maddie turned away from Trey then, unwilling to show him the face of that realization. She couldn't let him see her devastation. She walked over to the kitchen table and set his napkin in place. "W-we have lemon cake for dessert," she said quietly.

"Maddie?" he asked, clearly puzzled by her sudden change in demeanor. "Honey, are you okay?"

His sweet tone tore at her heart. Maddie wasn't good at subterfuge. She'd always been the what-you-see-is-what-you-get kind of girl. Afraid her voice would tremble when she spoke, she bobbed her head up and down.

"Okay," he said, unsure. "I'll catch a quick shower and be back in ten minutes."

She nodded again.

Once he exited the room, Maddie sighed with relief. She realized she had ten minutes to pull herself together. She couldn't let her feelings for Trey be known. It was imperative that, for however long she'd be living at 2 Hope Ranch she maintain the budding friendship she'd developed with Trey and keep it simple.

She'd fought a long hard battle and had lost.

She'd fallen in love with a man who couldn't love her back.

TREY FORKED HIS first bite of lemon cake and guided it into his mouth, savoring the pungent lemony flavor as it slid down his throat. He didn't know if it was the cake or the fact that Maddie had baked for him, but he'd never tasted anything better.

The best he'd ever had.

Trey stared at Maddie across the table, taking a bite of cake, chewing thoughtfully and realized how much he'd enjoyed walking into his kitchen after a day's work to find her there, waiting for him. She'd cast him a small timid smile, looking apprehensive and so pretty in her black dress with the table set and dinner cooking.

Good God, if he wasn't careful, he'd do something stupid, like ask her to stay on at Hope Wells, ask her to stay with him at the ranch.

An instant recollection came to mind of another "best" he'd ever had—the night they'd made love. He'd never wanted a woman more or experienced such intense lack of willpower. He'd lost all rational thought that night, allowing his natural instincts and raw desire to take over. He and Maddie had shared an incredible night, one he'd never forget.

Day in and day out, he fought his feelings for her, but still, he wanted her. Little Maddie Brooks, the animal doc, the petite, wholesome redhead who had knocked his world off-kilter.

He figured once she left Hope Wells, he could forget all about her. He figured with miles distancing them, he'd move on and so would she. She'd settle in at the new clinic in Denver, dive into her work, and most likely hook up with that Nick character.

Trey frowned, his lips pulling down the corners of his

mouth.

"Don't you like the cake?" Maddie asked.

She had misinterpreted his sour mood. Trey sent her a reassuring smile. "I was just thinking that you're spoiling me. Nobody's ever baked a better cake than this, Maddie."

"Really?" Her pensive mood lightened.

"It's the best I've—" he began, but halted immediately, noting Maddie's sharp gaze on him. He couldn't repeat the vow he'd spoken when they'd made love. The reminder would be too painful to both of them. "It's delicious."

He took another big bite, taking immense pleasure as he chewed.

Maddie played with a bit of frosting on her fork. "You could always ask Darla to bake you one."

Surprised, Trey nearly choked on a mouthful of food. "Darla?"

Maddie looked at him directly and nodded, her green eyes bright with curiosity. "Yes, Darla."

Trey laid his fork down and leaned back in his chair. "There's nothing between Darla and me anymore."

Maddie continued to look at him, waiting for more. Silently, Trey sighed, realizing that Maddie expected more of an explanation. He didn't like dredging up the past. Whenever he did, his recollections always proved what he knew in his heart to be true, that he wasn't cut out for relationships.

"We dated for a short time."

Maddie remained silent.

"Darla went through a pretty messy divorce. I think I was the first man she dated after her breakup. And well, in the beginning it was nice. We had a good time together. But then, Darla got serious about us and I started feeling closed in—like a vise grip crushing my neck. I felt lousy about doing so, but I broke it off."

"How did she take it?" Maddie asked.

"She wasn't happy, and I'd hurt yet another woman. I'd made another mistake. For the longest time I felt guilty about that. But last night, she cleared all that up for me."

"How?"

"She told me, plain as day, she hadn't been ready for a relationship. She'd admitted that our breakup was the best thing that could've happened to her. She'd needed time to straighten out her life. She's happier now than she's ever been. She has a long distance relationship with a man living in Dallas and that suits her just fine."

A small smile graced her lips. "And she's got five healthy pups and a new mama to keep her busy, too."

"Yeah, that, too."

"You must feel relieved. All this time you thought you'd hurt her and she came out better for it."

Trey couldn't agree. He'd entered into that relationship blindly, not realizing how vulnerable Darla would be after a terrible divorce. The potential for causing her pain had been there all along, but Darla had made her way through despite Trey's disregard for her feelings. "I bolted the minute things got too close for comfort, Maddie. There's no denying that."

Maddie's expression changed. She lost the beam in her eyes, the smile on her face. "Is that what happened between you and me? You got that closed-in feeling?"

"Hell, no." Trey shook his head and made a wide sweeping gesture with his arms. "With you, it was as if the whole world opened up, and I was right smack in the middle of it."

Maddie blinked.

"Damn it." He never wanted to admit that to her. He never wanted to give her reason to hope. Yet, something deep inside couldn't allow Maddie to think he'd used her that night. He couldn't allow her to think she'd suffocated him. Just the opposite was true. She'd made him feel alive and vital and open to all good things.

"I felt that way, too," she whispered.

Trey stood then and reached for her, guiding her up until she stood facing him. She looked so beautiful tonight, her sad green eyes catching the pale light. Trey couldn't resist holding her once more. He took her in his arms, splaying his hands around her tiny waist and spoke softly. "You're a dangerous woman, Maddie Brooks."

She stared at the collar of his shirt. "Do I scare you, Trey?"

Trey tipped her chin up with a finger and their eyes met. "More than you'll ever know." He bent down and kissed her on the lips. "So sweet."

"It's the frosting," she said softly.

He kissed her once again. "It's you, Maddie."

Maddie reached up and wrapped her arms around his neck, tugging him closer. The kiss went deeper this time and longer until the sugary sweet taste of Maddie was etched in his head for eternity.

In harmony, they both moaned, a quiet little plea that spoke of untold pleasure. Trey deepened the kiss further, driving his tongue in her mouth, mating with her in the most elemental way. Their bodies brushed once, then melded together perfectly as Maddie's soft supple form crushed against Trey's granite hard body.

Trey was at a loss to stop, his need for Maddie too great. He held her tight and kissed her passionately, igniting a spark that would surely burst into flames. He moved his hands to cup her bottom, molding her cheeks in his palms feeling the soft firm skin hidden under her dress. Spurred on by her tiny little whimpers, he caressed the delicate small of her back, making tiny circles and gliding his hands over her. He slid them up to stroke her shoulders, until finally his hands found the back of her head. He wove his fingers into the silky copper strands, aching for all of her, wanting to take her to bed and make love to her throughout the night. And just as he began to speak those words, she pulled away with a shake of her head. She broke off their connection.

Her eyes closed briefly and when she opened them her voice was soft, filled with sobering pain. "You're a better man than you think you are, Trey. I wish you could see that you have more staying power than most men I know."

He blinked his eyes.

Maddie didn't give him a chance to explain. She spun away and headed out of the room. He watched her go and each step she took to distance herself from him was a blunt rap to his gut.

Bereft, Trey didn't blame her for walking away. It was the right thing to do.

A man shouldn't dally with a woman like Maddie Brooks, yet that didn't stop his gut from spitting fire or his own heart from sorely aching.

Chapter Ten

"THAT'S A GOOD wild stallion." Maddie held a lead rope and walked with Storm along a path behind the ranch house. She'd finished work early and decided that a pleasant afternoon walk would do them both a world of good.

Maddie had made mistakes while living at 2 Hope Ranch, but she planned to rectify what she could. And Storm had been high on her list. She'd never come up against an animal with so much resistance. Normally Maddie could coax a horse to do her bidding, but not Storm. He was definitely and infinitely a stallion with his own obstinate mind.

While she thought she'd gained the horse's trust, she really hadn't. She'd rushed him, thinking the little leeway he'd given her had been enough. So now, Maddie used a different tactic. She didn't want to destroy the animal's spirit, only settle him somewhat.

"You're not so different than Trey, you know," she said, speaking freely along the path, with no worry of being overheard. "You're headstrong and feisty as all get out."

Maddie quietly chuckled, a good release for her pent-up frustration. Last night, she'd wanted Trey as much as he'd wanted her. But Maddie was a realist and understood that until Trey came to grips with his heritage and his past, she'd only be opening herself up to more heartache. As difficult as it was, she'd pushed Trey away last night for both of their sakes.

She moved along the path speaking in a level voice with patience and care, hoping to create a special bond with Storm, hoping he would learn to accept her. "And afterward, if you keep up this good behavior, I'll give you a nice rubdown, a soothing little massage for your muscles." Maddie worked out a kink in her shoulder. "I only wish you could reciprocate."

Maddie felt comfortable with this approach, taking small steps and bonding with the stallion as if he were hers. She understood Storm better now and realized he had a long way to go before he would relinquish his trust.

After thirty minutes, they headed back toward the ranch. She was satisfied that Storm hadn't rejected the interaction between them. The stallion actually seemed content. She walked Storm into the barn and headed for his paddock, the largest in the building. As they bypassed a docile bay mare named Julip, one of Trey's cutting horses, she slowed her steps carefully measuring Storm's reaction to the mare.

Maddie had spent time with this particular mare during her stay here and knew her sweet nature. As she led Storm to

Julip's stall the two horses came face to face.

Storm bristled, breathing out nosily, stomping his feet. Maddie's heart pumped hard, hoping she hadn't made a big mistake. Normally, Storm stayed outside in his corral, too unruly and quite frankly, too lusty, to be thrown in with female horses. But Julip merely stared at him, and if a horse could shrug and roll her eyes, Maddie was sure this mare had done just that. Julip turned her back on Storm and moved to the far end of her stall, clearly not impressed with the stallion.

To Maddie's amazement, Storm's little outburst nearly all but disappeared and she had to really tug on the rope she held to get Storm to move away from Julip's stall.

"Hmm. Interesting," Maddie said as an idea stirred around in her head.

"What's interesting?" Trey's low voice from behind gave her a start.

Maddie turned smoothly around, her moves cautious and slow, in deference to Storm's unpredictable nature. She stared into Trey's deep disapproving eyes. "Oh, nothing. Storm and I just went for a walk."

Trey's brows furrowed. He winced. "You went for a walk *alone* with him? Not a good idea, Maddie. I thought you'd learned your lesson."

Trey stood with hands on hips in his black Stetson, dark snap-down work shirt and leather-fringed chaps. Maddie took a swallow. Trey, darn him, always stole her breath when he caught her unaware. In that one second, before rational sense took hold, she'd envisioned a life with him at 2 Hope Ranch. A life without caution or trepidation tripping them up. A life filled with happiness.

She focused on the stallion instead of her silly notions, and gave him a gentle pat on the neck. "Storm and I came to an understanding."

Trey frowned. He wouldn't take his eyes off of Storm, as if he fully expected the horse to bolt. "Yeah? And what was that?"

"We had a nice walk and now I'm going to give him a rubdown."

Trey blinked. He pointed at Storm and lowered his voice. "You will not get in that stall with him, Maddie. To begin with, he's hardly ever in there. It's too confining for him. He won't like you invading his territory. You know well and good that he's more wild than tame."

"I think he's ready."

Trey folded his arms around his middle and dug in his boot heels. "No."

"No?"

"I forbid it." Trey grabbed the rope from Maddie's hands.

Shocked, Maddie repeated his words, "You forbid it?"

Trey nodded.

Maddie's eyes grew wide. Her face colored with heat and the hair at the nape of her neck stood on end. "You're forgetting that I'm an animal doctor, Trey. I know animals better than I know people. I can do this."

"He's not ready. He may never be ready, Maddie."

She planted her hands on her hips. "I disagree. He's pigheaded like you, but unlike you, he'll come around."

"Don't fight me on this, Maddie. I won't change my mind." Trey led Storm away, turning him around to head toward the opened barn door.

Maddie fumed silently. Normally she wouldn't be so bold. Trey owned Storm. He had the final say in his treatment and care. Maddie had no rights when it came to the stallion. But still, it irritated her that Trey wouldn't allow her this. He was as closed off as the first day she'd met him.

"Just who are you trying to protect?" Maddie muttered. And after Trey had left the barn entirely, she added, "Me or the stallion? Or maybe, yourself?"

MINUTES LATER, TREY stood by the fence watching Storm race around the perimeter of the corral, his jet-black mane flying in the fading sunlight. The stallion was too spirited to tame, and though Trey had immense respect for Maddie's abilities with animals, he couldn't allow her to place herself in danger. Storm needed gentling over a long period of time—he couldn't be rushed. No doubt, Maddie had goodness in her heart. She was a positive thinker, believing that she could change things that were unchangeable. But Trey knew better, learning his lessons firsthand. He and Maddie probably would never see eye to eye on the subject.

He'd been harsh with her in the barn, perhaps overly so, to make his point. But the truth remained that he couldn't abide Maddie getting hurt again. She'd already made one bad judgment call with the stallion the night of the dust storm. She'd been fortunate in not sustaining life-threatening injuries. So he figured that while he couldn't do anything about the emotional hurt he'd caused her lately, he'd damn well see to it that she wouldn't get hurt physically while living on his ranch.

Trey presumed she'd be packing her suitcase soon anyway, anxious to leave 2 Hope, anxious to leave *him.* He'd made one mistake after another with her. With all the best intentions, he'd tried protecting her and wound up hurting her in the process. She'd be better off without him.

Much better off.

A car pulled up, kicking up dry dust and coming to a stop right next to him. Trey turned to find his cousin Jack exiting his patrol car wearing his tan sheriff's uniform and a big smile. "Howdy, Trey."

Trey wasn't in the mood for Jack's good humor. "Hey, Jack. What's up? Are you on duty or is this a social call?"

Jack glanced around, searching the property. "Maddie around?"

"You came out here to see Maddie?" Trey asked, masking

his irritation the best he could. Jack didn't seem to notice, his gaze kept darting around the borders of the ranch.

"Nope. I came out here to see you." He grinned and Trey's irritation grew at Jack's mysterious behavior. "So, where is she?"

Trey shrugged. "She's probably in her office, working."

Jack glanced toward the old barn. "Good. I'm here on a mission. Caroline's throwing Maddie a surprise birthday party this Saturday night. She asked me to come over here to let you know about it. She didn't want to risk having Maddie overhear the conversation."

"It's her birthday?"

"Not until next week. She'll be twenty-eight and Caroline is dead serious about keeping this a surprise. That's why she's doing it early. She has this idea to get her over to her place. She wants you to bring her."

"Me? How am I supposed to do that?"

Jack smiled. "She wants you to ask her out to dinner, so Maddie will dress up pretty and be ready. Caroline figured she'd call with a baby-sitting emergency asking Maddie to come over to watch Annabelle for half an hour before your date. The rest of us will be there waiting."

Trey began shaking his head. "No. I can't do that."

"Sure you can."

"No, I can't."

"You can't?" Jack wore his stubborn Walker expression. Trey recognized the tightening of his mouth, the set of his jaw. He'd worn that same expression more than a few times himself. "Well, why the hell not?"

Trey confessed, "Because I doubt Maddie would go anywhere with me."

Jack pursed his lips and eyed him with doubt. "I don't believe it. You two have been hot for each other since she moved in with you."

"Believe it," Trey said firmly.

Jack sighed. "What happened?"

Trey refused Jack the details. He didn't need to know how Maddie's coming to live with him had been the best and worst time in his life. He didn't need to know that they lived in turmoil, Trey making one mistake after another with her. He didn't need to know how much Trey cared about her, willing to do whatever it took to keep her safe and protected. Hell, Trey had just come to that conclusion himself. "Doesn't matter. Maddie's not speaking to me."

Jack's expression changed to a full out grin. "She's not?"

Trey cursed. "You don't have to be so damn happy about it."

"I'm not," Jack said, adjusting his expression accordingly. "But I'm sure if you turned on the Walker charm, you could get her to go out with you."

Trey shrugged. "Even if that were true, I'm not going to do it. It's best this way. Caroline is just going to have to figure another way to get Maddie over there."

"The party's in five days, Trey. That doesn't give her

much time. And why is it best that you don't ask her out?"

Trey shrugged again. "She'll be leaving soon. I'm sure of it. Moving to Denver is a great opportunity for her." And he wouldn't be around to hurt her any longer. He wouldn't have to yearn for a woman he couldn't have.

"So, you're refusing?"

Trey nodded. "It's for the best. Trust me."

Jack removed his hat and rubbed the back of his neck, contemplating. "I'm going to have to ask her myself then. Caroline trusted me with this, and I'm not going to let her down." Jack's mouth pulled down in a frown. "You think she's mad enough at you to agree to go out with me?"

Trey searched Jack's eyes. He could see his cousin's reluctance, but Trey had put him in a bad position. All in all, Trey realized Jack wanted what was best for him and as much as his cousin had teased and tormented, he wasn't eager to ask Maddie out. "If you ask her today, she'd probably join you on a trip to the moon."

"All right," Jack said on a sigh, before turning toward Maddie's office. "Hell, Trey. Sometimes, you are your own worst enemy."

MADDIE EXITED THE barn with Julip all saddled up and ready for a ride. She needed the distraction and this little outing would help take her mind off the Walker men. They had confounded and confused her enough for an entire lifetime. She was barely speaking to Trey, and just minutes ago, Jack had asked her out. She'd been quite stunned by his invitation to the Sheriff Department's Annual Benefit dinner, but he'd been so sweet and sincere, promising they'd not call it a date, but merely dinner with a friend. Maddie couldn't see any harm in going, so she had agreed.

"That's a girl," she said, stroking the horse's forelock and patting her neck before mounting, happy to simply concentrate on a nice afternoon ride. Once in the saddle, she leaned down and gave Julip one last gentle stroke. "You're the sweetest little lady at 2 Hope."

She rode toward the corral, keeping a safe distance from Storm, and watched the stallion's reaction. She'd had a hunch about Storm and this experiment would prove whether she'd been right or not. The stallion raced to the fence snorting into the air, digging in and sifting dirt with his hooves until he received what he seemed to want, the mare's attention. Julip gave the stallion a glance. She was not intimated or interested and Maddie grinned. She admired Julip's nonchalance with the blustering male.

Maddie missed working with Storm and had stayed away for two days, keeping busy with her own work and trying to forget about her heated conversation with Trey the other day. She kept telling herself he'd been within his rights. He owned the stallion, and she had to respect his wishes.

But Maddie didn't have to like it. It seemed that she and

Trey butted heads more than got along these days. But she knew she could get through to Storm. She knew she could get him to trust, without breaking his spirit. And the sweet-natured Julip would be the one to help her.

She guided the mare slowly around the perimeter of the corral, several yards away from the fence. Julip seemed to enjoy the exercise and paid Storm and his initial tirade little mind. They made the turn once, then twice, as Storm watched on from his stance inside the corral.

Maddie continued to keep the mare's pace slow. Then on the third trip around the corral, Storm approached the fence and moved along with them from inside the corral. As any dominant stallion would, he took a slight lead rearing his head up as if to say, follow me.

"That's it, boy," Maddie said softly. They continued on this way until Maddie felt it safe enough to guide Julip closer to the perimeter of the fence. The two horses trotted nearly beside each other now, separated only by the fence.

"That's a different approach," Kit said, minutes later as Maddie dismounted Julip in front of the barn. "I gotta hand it to you, you don't give up. Nobody around here ever thought that stallion was worth the money Trey paid for it. We all sorta thought the boss made himself a bull-size mistake. But now," Kit said, taking off his hat to scratch his head, "seeing the progress you're making I'm thinking it wasn't but a little bitty mistake."

Maddie chuckled and patted the mare's rump. "I can't

take all the credit. Julip is just what Storm needs."

Kit glanced at Storm, kicking up another ruckus inside the corral. "Maybe so. Maybe what you're doing is a good thing. Seems the right female could tame the wild out of any male."

The sound of a truck's engine had both of them turning their heads. Trey pulled up and parked his car on the side of the house. He climbed out of the cab, pushed his hat further up his forehead and glanced their way.

Kit waved at his boss. "Maybe you just might have what it takes to settle him."

"I hope so," Maddie said, still reeling from the success of her little experiment.

"And I wasn't exactly talking about the stallion." Kit tipped his hat and winked.

Maddie's mouth dropped open but Kit had walked off before she could utter a word.

"Tell me why you feel the need to shop, again?" Maddie asked Caroline. She needed convincing that she should be carousing around in boutiques on her afternoon off. Not that she didn't love spending time with Caroline, she always did. But shopping wasn't on her list of priorities at the moment.

She and Caroline entered a trendy boutique and began

perusing a rack of summertime dresses. "Because you have a hot date with Jack Walker, that's why," Caroline answered. "We need to find you a special outfit."

Maddie frowned and Caroline quickly added, "And I need a day away from sandboxes and playgroups. I need a girl's day out."

"Just to set the record straight, it's not a hot date, Caroline." She'd never have agreed to go out with Jack if she thought he wanted more than friendship. "Jack asked me to this benefit dinner for the sheriff's department. He made it clear that we'd go as friends."

Caroline shot her a knowing smile. "The old 'just friends' line. Tell me, how is it that you've got both of the Walker men interested in you? First Trey, now Jack."

Maddie glanced at a pretty yellow-and-black two-piece silk suit, before addressing her friend. "First of all, Trey and I are barely speaking. And Jack, well, he's a sweetheart, but we really are just friends."

"Hmm." Caroline's blond brows rose in doubt.

"Really. I could never . . . I mean Jack is Trey's cousin and—"

"I hear what you're saying. You can't take Jack seriously. It's always been Trey for you. Too bad, he's so hung up on his past."

Maddie lifted a flowery sundress off the rack and placed it under her chin, glancing in the mirror. "It isn't just *his* past he's fighting, but generations of Walker men."

Caroline shook her head at Maddie's choice. "Oh no, not that."

She set the dress back on the rack, relying on Caroline's good judgment.

"I'm hoping that maybe one day Trey will wake up and see that he's not the man his father was," Maddie said. "Trey's really a decent man."

"I'm hoping you're still around when he finally does wake up. Have you made up your mind about Nick's job offer?"

"I'm still thinking it through. He's been so patient with me. I spoke with him yesterday and promised I would give him my answer by next week."

"Don't go," Caroline blurted, then covered her mouth with her hand. "Sorry. I shouldn't have said that."

Maddie smiled sadly. This decision would change her entire life. She'd just settled in Hope Wells, having made some truly wonderful friends. Her practice was growing and if she decided to rebuild her office here, she wouldn't have a problem making ends meet. She truly liked living in Hope Wells, but she often wondered how difficult it would be to live in a small town and bump into Trey from time to time. How difficult would it be to see him move on with his life—to see him with another woman?

Sometimes, accepting Nick's proposal and moving to Denver made all the sense in the world. And at other times, like right now, as she stared into the sweet, caring eyes of her best friend, moving away wasn't even a possibility.

"Caroline, you don't have to be sorry. I understand. I'd miss you and Annabelle so much if I left but—"

"You have much more to consider. You're talented and intelligent and that Denver clinic would be lucky to have you. Tell me, what does that stubborn cowboy have to say about you leaving?"

Maddie stared at her latest selection, deciding the dress wasn't right and hung it back on the rack. With a deep sigh, she turned to her friend, her ragged emotions catching her by surprise. Misty-eyed, she spoke quietly, "Let me put it this way, I think it'd be easier on both of us if I left."

"Oh, Maddie."

Maddie shrugged and Caroline put her arm around her as they exited the shop.

"Hey, I know what you need," Caroline said after a minute of silence, her voice light, filled with whimsy. "We'll worry about a new dress later. What you need is sexy lingerie!"

Maddie stared at her friend for a moment and then a bubble of silly laughter escaped. "What?"

"Trust me. When I was going through my heartache with Gil, nothing perked me up more than buying something soft and feminine and . . . *sinful.*"

"Sinful?" The notion began growing on her. Why not indulge and have some real fun shopping with her friend. Maddie's life lately was all too serious. "You know, I like that idea. I'm feeling better already."

"There. You see what I mean. Just wait until we find you something sensational. You'll feel so sexy you won't have a care in the world."

"Sounds good to me. But where do we find this sensational something?"

"Not in Hope Wells, that's for sure. I know this place..."

WITH SUNLIGHT FADING on the horizon, Trey walked into the house and hung his hat on a peg in the kitchen. He sighed. At least he'd been able to catch up on some of his chores. They seemed to be mounting every day. The doggone barn roof had started leaking thanks to the last T-storm, fences were down on the south pasture, and he had to check on his livestock. One mama cow was almost ready to drop her calf. He moved her into a barn stall just minutes ago, vowing to check on her every hour or so.

Trey opened the refrigerator, grabbed a Coors and took one long, swig. The beer refreshed his parched throat and lent him some measure of comfort. He'd taken to avoiding Maddie whenever possible lately. Now, damn it, his little plan was backfiring. She was on his mind constantly. He missed her like crazy.

She'd been a breath of fresh air, a sweet-natured, strong-willed woman who had brought his mundane ranch to vibrant life. And as he tipped his bottle and took another swig, forcing his thoughts from Maddie Brooks, out of the corner of his eye he spotted a light-pink shopping bag tipped over on the entry table. The contents had spilled out in a frilly heap on the plank wood floor.

Curious, Trey strode over to the antique table and set his beer down next to the pink bag that read with delicate black letters, *Double-Dare.* He bent on one knee and lifted a garment up. Panties?

His breath caught as he fingered the lace panties, tracing over a black stitched rose strategically placed on the front. Man oh man. He gulped air.

Carefully, he placed the panties back in the bag. He picked up the next two items, a matched set attached by a transparent cord. The tag read, Embroidered Demi-Bra and Bikini Panties. Red/Nude. The bra and panties were sheer except for a patch of crimson embroidery. Trey's imagination ran wild, picturing what the embroidery was meant to hide on Maddie's sexy little body.

He took a swallow. His mouth was as dry as a rolling tumbleweed. His mind wandered to secret places he normally didn't visit. What would Maddie's soft, creamy skin look like encased in tantalizing red?

He would love to know.

So Maddie Brooks was a woman who enjoyed wearing sexy lingerie. The idea contrasted greatly with the day-to-day professional image she exhibited while on the ranch. He remembered her wearing a thong, and now this peek into her nighttime wild side turned him on big time. There was no denying that. Trey gave the bra and panties one last look then shoved them into the bag.

One item to go. Trey picked it up and read the label. Lace Babydoll/Vintage Look. The mauve nightie plunged at the neckline and dipped so deep that Trey wondered why in hell they even bothered. He inhaled sharply, noting that the short hem would hardly cover what needed covering, but then wasn't that the intent?

Trey stared at the nightie, his heart in his throat, his groin growing tight. He visualized running his palms over the soft lace, caressing her breasts, then moving his hands lower, testing the thong with his fingers until both of them were ready to combust.

He remembered Maddie so well, the heat of her body, the smell of her skin, the flaming burn of their lovemaking. So when the front door opened and Maddie entered, Trey couldn't mask the lust on his face. He wouldn't even try.

"T-Trey?"

She stood over him in mild shock, her hair in disarray, her face smudged with dirt, her jeans coated with straw and grass stains. She looked a wreck, so much so that Trey had to smile. He had to because he loved her so damn much, that he saw past all of that to the beautiful, sexy, perfect woman underneath. He loved her so damn much that his heart burned clear through his chest. She was the woman he wanted beyond life itself. The woman he wouldn't hurt and could never have.

"What are you doing with my . . . things?"

Trey lifted the baby doll up. "You mean these? I found them on the floor when I walked in. The bag had tipped over."

"And you were nice enough to pick them up?"

Trey shook his head and stood, still holding the nightie. "Honey, there was nothing *nice* about what I was thinking."

Even through the dirt on her face, Trey noticed her blush. He placed that last garment into the bag. "Did you leave them for me to see?"

Maddie's face colored again, this time with anger. She grabbed the bag from his hand. "I had an emergency call the minute I walked through the door. I must have set the bag down there without realizing it."

Trey scrubbed his jaw, contemplating. "Makes sense. So, did you buy them for your date with Jack?"

Maddie closed her eyes and cursed. Trey had never heard her use such language and when she opened her eyes, staring deeply into his, she spoke quietly. "I *bought them* for no one in particular. And it's not a date, just dinner with a friend."

"Are you sure about that?"

Maddie shook her head and ran a hand through her disheveled hair. Her eyes clouded in frustration. Hell, he was frustrated too. "Trey, what do you want from me?"

Everything. "Nothing, Maddie."

"When I walked in here a minute ago, it didn't look like you wanted nothing. It looked as though you had something *definite* on your mind."

"What do you want me to say?" he rushed out "That even dirt-stained and muddied up, you're prettier than any woman I've ever laid eyes on? That I held those sexy clothes in my hands and envisioned you wearing them for me? That I want you, with or without that fancy lingerie, regardless of how much you'd end up being hurt in the end. All that's true, Maddie. But I'm not going to do it. I told you once before, wanting you and doing right by you are two different things."

Maddie bit down on her lip, brilliant green sparks flashed in her eyes. "Maybe the wanting and doing right by me are one and the same, Trey. Maybe you're all wrong about us. Have you ever considered that?"

Trey shook his head. "No. I'm not wrong."

The Walker Curse still plagued him. He'd never get out from under the genetic scar that deprived him of faith and trust. Maddie was a keeper. He'd known that from the very start. She deserved more than the heartache he'd send her way one day.

"Are you sure about that?" She tossed that question back in his face.

Damn it. No, he wasn't sure of anything anymore. Maddie had hinted, cajoled and insinuated that Trey was a better man than he thought he was. And all of her sweet-talking had worked its way into his head, making him wonder. It gave him hope.

"Think about it, Trey." She walked out of the room, hugging to her chest the shopping bag filled with sexy lingerie that Trey would never see again.

Chapter Eleven

"Maybe I should cancel my plans with Jack," Maddie said, as she glanced at the laboring cow. She stood with Trey in the maternity stall they'd concocted of sand and sawdust to help the cow deliver safely.

"That's not necessary," Trey said, shaking his head. "I've delivered more than my fair share of calves. This one isn't going to be as difficult as we'd thought. You said so yourself. She's doing a great job on her own."

Maddie took another glance at the cow straining to deliver her young one. By all means, Trey was right. The cow would probably do fine, but part of Maddie's handshake contract with Trey was to oversee his livestock and silly as it seemed, she felt guilty leaving Trey to deal with the cow while she went out for dinner. She felt guilty, even through her anger at him. It had taken her days to recover from Trey's obstinate behavior regarding Storm. And she finally realized that it did them both no good to be at odds. She wasn't one for holding grudges. "I know you're right, but—"

"No buts, Maddie. I'm right."

Trey had the confidence of twenty men when it came to

ranching dilemmas. Sadly, he just didn't have much confidence in himself when it came to commitment. So instead of Maddie spending Saturday night enjoying his company, she'd agreed to spend the evening with his cousin.

"Won't Jack be picking you up soon?" he asked.

"Yes, in less than an hour. How come you know so much about my plans?" Maddie asked, baffled by Trey's obvious nonchalance over her date with Jack.

She expected him to be more... something. Yet he didn't seem annoyed or upset or jealous. Maddie's ego had been bruised in the past from a lackluster love life, but never more than her time here at 2 Hope Ranch. Never more than in her dealings with Trey.

There were times when Trey would look at her like she was the only woman on the planet and her heart would soar with anticipation. His hungry stares spoke of steamy nights ahead, but ever since the one time they'd been together, Trey hadn't acted upon the heated looks he cast her. She knew he fought an inner battle. She knew he struggled with demons that had existed before they'd ever met. Yet, Maddie hoped she'd broken through his defenses. She wanted to make a difference in his life.

"Jack squared it with me."

"He asked *your* permission?"

Trey let out a wry chuckle. "Hardly. More like he told me his plans, point blank." He frowned and added, "Whether I liked it or not."

It meant something to Maddie that Trey didn't sound happy about her date with Jack, but she wouldn't explain her reasons for going. She liked Jack and he seemed so sincere when he'd asked her to go to this benefit with him as a friend. "Well, I'd better get dressed. But if the cow—"

"I'll come get you if there's a problem."

"Promise?"

Trey nodded. "Promise."

Maddie headed for the shower and once done she dried and curled her hair. She'd decided on a soft peach summertime dress with a frilly flounce at the hem. The dress wasn't overly fancy, something she'd picked up at a local shop, but a new pair of earrings and matching necklace brought the whole outfit together quite nicely.

She put on a pair of lacy sandals, grabbed her purse and exited the room, dressing in record time so she could take a moment to check on the laboring cow. The knock came just as Maddie had reached the front door. She opened it to find Jack standing on the porch, wearing a chocolate brown western suit, the exact color of his eyes. Clean-shaven and well groomed, Jack smiled. Gosh, he was handsome and that cocky grin was enough to make most women swoon. There was nothing ordinary about Walker men—every last one she'd met was as handsome as the devil himself.

"Wow," he said, his eyes flickering over her. "You look great."

Maddie gave him a smile. "So do you, Jack. You're handsome in your uniform, but even more so out of it."

Jack's brows rose as he chuckled.

"Oh, I didn't mean it that way. You know wh—"

Her cell phone rang at that awkward moment and Maddie glanced at name popping up on the screen. "It's Caroline," she told Jack, leaving the door open so he could come inside. "Excuse me for one second."

She walked into the kitchen to answer the call privately and spoke with her friend. Caroline needed a favor. But Maddie had to double-check with Jack to make sure it was doable. "Hang on a second," she said and walked into the room to explain to Jack.

"Caroline is in a bind. She needs help with Annabelle. Do you think we could stop over to her house to watch Annabelle for half an hour? The babysitter has to leave and Caroline doesn't think she'll make it back from town in time. I know it's a huge favor, and I certainly don't want to make us late for the benefit, but Caroline really needs the help."

Jack glanced at his watch. "Not a problem at all. The dinner doesn't start until eight. We have more than enough time."

"Oh, good," Maddie said. She was happy she didn't have to refuse helping Caroline. She made the call brief. "Yes, we can make it. Jack said we have plenty of time. We'll be right over."

She hung up from Caroline and smiled at Jack, who was

waiting for her by the door. He was such a good guy. Why hadn't she fallen for him instead of Trey? Everything seemed simple with Jack. He was easy to talk to, easy to be with, and he certainly didn't entertain any thoughts of the Walker Curse.

"Thank you," she said, closing the door behind them. "You're a saint."

Jack opened the car door for her. "That isn't the way most people would describe me."

"How do people describe you?" she asked curious.

He leaned against the car door and cocked his mouth up. "Pretty much as a big pain in the ass. My only redeeming quality is my sense of humor, odd that it is. And my deep sense of loyalty. That's why my family puts up with me."

"Because you're loyal?"

"Nah, because I make them laugh."

And Maddie laughed as she slid into her seat. Jack closed the door and climbed into the driver's seat beside her. He started the engine just as Maddie saw Trey exiting the barn. Their gazes met over the distance of the yard. He gave her a reassuring nod. Maddie immediately understood. All had gone well with the calf's delivery.

Maddie sighed with relief. Jack turned the car around and headed out the gate toward Caroline's house.

"Annabelle's no trouble at all," Maddie explained to Jack as they climbed up the Portman's front steps a few minutes later. "And I'm sure Caroline will be along any minute."

Maddie knocked on the door and a young girl answered. "Hello. You must be Sherry. I'm Maddie Brooks, Caroline's friend and this is Jack Walker. We're your reinforcements."

"Hi. Come in." The young girl smiled warmly and let them in.

Maddie took two steps into the house and stopped, bumping into Jack as a swarm of smiling faces popped out of nowhere and chorused. "Surprise!"

Jack held her shoulders steady and chuckled. "Happy Birthday, Maddie."

She blinked and looked at multicolored helium balloons eating up the two far corners of the room, a line of crepe paper decorations hanging from end to end and a giant-size birthday sign on the wall above the fireplace. "B-birthday?" she repeated.

She'd put her upcoming birthday out of her mind and would've never suspected a party, much less, a *surprise.* Her friends gathered around her, giving her hugs and wishing her happy birthday.

After the congratulations died down, Caroline approached wearing an ear-to-ear grin. "Happy Birthday, dear friend." Her arms wrapped around Maddie's shoulders and she hugged tight. Their embrace lasted long enough for Maddie to fully comprehend what Caroline had done for her.

"I had no idea," Maddie said. Tears pooled in her eyes. "This is so . . . so amazing." She wiped at her lower eyelashes with her finger, hoping mascara wasn't staining her face.

The hem of her dress was given a few yanks. Distracted, Maddie looked down. Little Annabelle, the adorable culprit dressed in her Sunday best, was smiling. Maddie bent to pick her up. "Hi sweetie." She gave her a loving squeeze.

"Did we surprise you?" Annabelle asked.

"Oh, yes. You and Mommy did a good job of surprising me."

"I helped Mommy do decorating."

"You did a perfect job. Everything is beautiful."

Maddie swept her gaze at the guests again, this time really seeing each and every one. Jack, of course, had taken a place next to his father, Monty. Both men grinned at her with twinkling eyes. Kit and his wife stood behind them, along with Brittany and Paul and half a dozen of Maddie's closest and dearest clients, people she had come to know very well by treating their animals. Even Darla was here and behind her stood a man, who began to make his way out from the small group.

Maddie set Annabelle down. "Nick!"

He reached her in three strides, and Maddie jumped up into his arms. She was touched that he'd come back to Hope Wells for her birthday. She didn't think she'd see him again so soon. He was swamped with his new enterprise.

"I just walked in ten minutes before you did. I almost didn't make it in time," Nick said.

She grinned like a silly fool. "I can't believe you're here, but I'm so glad that you are."

"So am I." Nick kissed her cheek. "Happy Birthday."

Overwhelmed and filled with joy, Maddie spent the better part of the hour making her rounds, speaking with all of the guests and picking at the food on her plate. Caroline had outdone herself, offering up a dinner buffet fit for a queen. And that's exactly how Maddie felt, like royalty tonight. Everything was perfect except . . .

Trey wasn't here.

She stared at the front door for the tenth time tonight. Would he show up?

"He's supposed to come," Jack said, in a rare serious tone. "He said he would."

Mortified that Jack had read her thoughts, Maddie fumbled. "Oh, I, uh . . . I was just wondering if he—"

"He knows about it. He didn't say he *wasn't* coming."

Maddie nodded. Why did it hurt so much that Trey hadn't bothered to come to her party? Why was she expecting to see him walk through that door flashing his killer smile and wishing her a happy birthday?

If she allowed it, her disappointment would swallow her up and make her seem ungrateful to all the wonderful people who had shown up, who had been kind and gracious to her throughout the year. Each and every one of them meant something special to her. Each, in their own way, defined Hope Wells, the small town with the big heart.

She glanced at Nick, who was laughing with Darla at the

moment and wondered if she belonged in Hope Wells at all. Should she finally make her decision to leave town?

Getting in on the ground floor of a new progressive clinic was an opportunity that came around only once in a lifetime. Those thoughts swept across her mind at intervals during each day, and each day the temptation seemed greater. It was like a magnet that pulled her in the direction of Denver. Whenever she really weighed her options, Trey Walker's image would pop into her head to confuse her and perhaps blind her to the possibilities.

"Hey, no pickle-pusses around here." Jack made a lighthearted jab at her jaw. "It's time for cake." He took her hand and led her into the dining area, and Maddie let thoughts of Trey ebb from her mind. She had friends here and she wanted to enjoy their company.

Hours later Jack pulled up in front of the house at 2 Hope. "It was a wonderful evening." Maddie sighed.

"I'm glad you had a good time."

"I did." She turned toward Jack and met with his mischievous eyes. "You're a good friend, Jack Walker. Even if you lied through your teeth to get me there."

Jack laughed. "You don't know how much I hate lying, but I had to. Trey wouldn't do . . . uh, never mind."

Maddie sat up straight in the seat and stared at him. "Trey? Was he supposed to bring me?"

"Uh, well . . . doggone it, Maddie. Sometimes my cousin is just a big jackass. Emphasis on *ass*."

Maddie squeezed her eyes shut. "It's okay, Jack."

"No, it's not okay. Hell, if you weren't head over heels about Trey, I'd be asking you out day and night. He's a damn fool, Maddie. But in his defense, he thinks this is best for you. He really cares about you."

Maddie glanced at the house, noting that Trey's light was still on. "I know he does." And that was why it hurt so darn much. She feared Trey had deliberately stayed away tonight, for her sake.

"Don't let it spoil your birthday."

"Oh, I won't. I see everything clearly now. If anything, this has helped me make a tough decision."

Maddie leaned over to kiss Jack on the cheek. "Thank you for being a wonderful friend."

Jack smiled. "Anytime."

He helped her out of the car first and then balanced boxes of her birthday gifts in his arms as he walked her to the door. "Want me to bring them in for you?"

Maddie shook her head. "No thanks. I've got everything under control."

She *did* have everything under control.

She sighed as she entered the house alone.

Her big decision was finally made.

HALF AN HOUR later, and twenty minutes past midnight,

Maddie stood bravely behind Trey's bedroom door. In her hands, she held a small square white box with a card that read:

Happy Birthday, Maddie.

Love, Trey

Her eyes had misted immediately upon seeing this small gift lying on her bed, a tied bunch of wildflowers eloquently crossing over the box. She immediately recognized the flowers as the ones that had sprouted up in a patch near the barn. She'd passed them every day, never really paying attention to their vivid color or sweet scent.

Her tears fell freely when she'd opened the box Trey had left for her. He'd given her a bracelet. It was an exact, nearly flawless replica of Aphrodite. The silver shone more brilliantly, but the bracelet matched her Grandma Mae's necklace perfectly.

Maddie had never received a more thoughtful gift.

"Oh, Trey," she whispered, standing behind his door with a rapidly beating heart, wishing things had turned out differently.

She knocked once, her hands trembling. "Trey, it's Maddie."

He opened the door seconds later, his dark hair swept back from his face. He wore jeans that dipped below his waist and nothing else. Maddie's breath hitched at the magnificence of his broad shoulders, the luster of his tanned chest. She hadn't forgotten the salty all-male taste of his skin, the granite hard feel of his body pressed against hers. Her mind flooded with memories of making love with him, of being as close as two people could possibly get. They'd shared more than body heat and desire. Their hearts had bonded together and no matter what Trey said or did Maddie knew that bond to be real and true.

"May I come in?" she asked and Trey opened the door wide to allow her entrance.

She stepped into the middle of his room and swiveled to look into the depths of his dark eyes. "I, uh, wanted to tell you, that I've made my decision about leaving for Denver."

Trey swallowed and took a deep breath, nodding his head. "I figured."

There was no question in his eyes, and no regret, either. Just resolute resignation. He didn't ask her intentions, and Maddie couldn't bring herself to discuss her decision. Tonight wasn't the time. Trey's bedroom wasn't the place.

"And I wanted to thank you for this." She opened the box she held and lifted out the bracelet. "It came as quite a surprise. The whole night has been full of surprises," she said in earnest. "But this . . . it's the most precious gift I've ever received. I'll treasure it as much as I'll treasure my time here with . . . my time here at 2 Hope." She handed him the bracelet. "Will you put it on me?"

His large, work-roughened hands fumbled a bit trying to undo the clasp. He leaned in to get a better look and they bumped heads. Both chuckled awkwardly and when he gazed into her eyes, Maddie knew she couldn't leave his room tonight. She couldn't sleep her last night at 2 Hope alone, when Trey was only a few rooms away.

"There," he said, taking her hand and turning it to admire the bracelet. "It fits."

His slight touch sent shivers throughout her defenseless body. Maddie smiled up into his eyes. "It does—a perfect match to my necklace."

"The jeweler used a sketch I'd made and well . . . he did a pretty darn good job."

Maddie touched Trey's cheek with one hand. "You went to all that trouble for me?"

He shrugged a shoulder, in that same way he had of brushing off a compliment. He spoke softly, "No one's more deserving than you."

Staring directly into his eyes, she didn't doubt his sincerity. Tears she'd thus far held back, fell one at a time, slowly, trickling down her face. "It's the best gift I've ever received, but it's not enough, Trey. I guess I'm a greedy woman, because I want more."

Maddie unzipped her dress, allowing the material to skim over her hips and down her body. She stepped out of it, her gaze never leaving Trey's eyes. She stood before him in her strappy sandals and newly purchased bold red underwear. "I want one last parting gift. One more night with you, Trey Walker."

Chapter Twelve

TREY'S HEART SLAMMED into his chest seeing Maddie's tearstained face, realizing that this would be her last night at 2 Hope. This would be their last night together. He'd always known that Maddie wouldn't stay. Hell, he'd done everything in his power to push her away.

And it worked.

She planned on leaving.

But Trey couldn't push her away tonight. Hell, he didn't have *that* much willpower, not when every cell in his body cried out for her. Not when he ached to hold her in his arms, kiss her adorable heart-shaped mouth and caress her smooth porcelain skin. How could he possibly deny her a last request when he wanted the same?

In the morning he'd wake up broken as a shattered shell of a man who would feel the loss of her leaving for a long time to come. But that didn't matter because she would move on to something better. She'd carve out the life she'd always wanted. She'd be free of him and the heartache he'd caused her.

He looked at her sweet expectant face and then followed

the lines of her body along each alluring curve and hollow. He made a complete and thorough sweep.

"Like I said before, I'd want you with or *without* those sexy things. You're beautiful, Maddie."

Maddie cast him a coy smile. "Without?"

Trey smiled and took her into his arms, pressing her body up to his. Her hands grazed his bare chest then moved up to circle his neck. His groin tightened and his heart pounded like a schoolboy being granted his first kiss. "There's time for *without*. I sorta like the *with*, for now." He toyed with the crimson strap of her bra. "Did you wear them for your party?"

Maddie lifted up on tiptoes and kissed his lips softly, but far too quickly. "No, I put them on afterward. For you."

"God, Maddie. You're killing me. You know that?" This time, he bent his head and kissed her, a hot exploration of lips and tongues with bodies meshed together and hearts pounding.

Without another word, Trey took her hand and led her to his bed. He sat down then gestured for her to sit next to him. "I've dreamt of making love to you here, sweetheart."

"I was only a few steps away," she whispered.

"Don't I know it."

Moonlight streamed in, casting her in a soft glow. Trey had always thought Maddie in the moonlight to be a beautiful thing, but never more than tonight. Light shimmered on her fiery hair, framing her pretty face and bringing a lustrous sheen to her smooth skin.

"It was all I could do to keep from coming for you in the middle of the night."

Maddie's eyebrows lifted with uncertainty. "Really?"

"Don't doubt it. It put me in more than one sour mood in the morning."

"Trey, why didn't you?"

"Shh." He placed a finger to her lips. "You know why, but let's not go there tonight, okay?"

She nodded and he kissed her softly on the lips. "We've wasted so much time," she whispered.

"And all we have is tonight."

Trey leaned back against the bed pillows, making room for Maddie. He took her hand and turned her toward him. She climbed on the bed and straddled his thighs. She made a sexy picture in her lingerie, so pretty, so unabashed in her trust of him. Her palms flattened on his chest, her slightest touch creating hot molten embers on his flesh. The burn was almost too much. Her tentative explorations made him grit his teeth, he wanted her so badly.

She toyed with his chest hairs, wrapping them around her slender fingers teasing him with tiny tugs and quick touches. Softly she sighed and the tempting sound echoed in his ears. Trey thought he would die from the pleasure.

She leaned down to kiss his lips, her thighs rubbing his, her torso tight against him, her red-lace-encased breasts crushing his chest. A groan erupted from his throat. A granite erection pressed the tight confines of his jeans and made him ache.

Maddie broke their lips apart and moved lower down on his body. She kissed his throat, his shoulders and his torso, then with her moist, perfect tongue she encircled his nipples and suckled.

"Damn, Maddie," he uttered, barely containing another groan.

To Trey, everything with Maddie had been about his self control. He'd resisted her for so long and right now, all he wanted to do was flip her onto her back and love her, driving them both over the edge until they were sated and spent. He wanted it all with Maddie. He wanted her to take her pleasure and give pleasure all night long. He wanted their last night together to be perfect. "I'm about to bust out of these here jeans, honey."

Maddie glanced down and shot him the sexiest, dewy-eyed look Trey had ever seen. It didn't help matters. His willpower was cresting.

She gestured to his zipper. "Want me to . . . uh."

"Yeah," he uttered, "although that might make it worse."

"But in a good way," she said. She slipped off him long enough to unzip his jeans and remove his boxers. Relief came quickly when he sprung free.

Maddie cupped his manhood, and Trey jerked and gritted his teeth.

They faced each other in the darkness as she moved her

hands on manhood, gliding up and down the shaft effortlessly.

He kissed her again and again as she turned his boring, lonely world completely upside down.

A minute of amazing torture later, Trey grabbed her hand and held her still. "How about we do the *without* now?"

Maddie chuckled softly as he reached around and unfastened her bra.

"The *without* is pretty damn good, too, sweetheart," he said, gazing at her. He tossed the bra aside and cupped her breast. The soft globe molded in his palm and he sucked in a deep breath. Leaning closer, he brought his mouth down to kiss the rosy-tipped crest.

Maddie moaned and wiggled her body. Trey continued to kiss her, using his tongue to moisten each nipple and then suckle gently until she was hot and wet from his lusty caresses. "So beautiful."

There would never be another woman in his life like Maddie Brooks. She was intelligent and wholesome, funny and sexy, innocent and bold as can be. Trey liked the way she gave all of herself to him. He liked the daring side of her. She'd been the best sex partner he'd ever had and she'd probably hold that title for the rest of his life. Hell, there wasn't one damn thing he didn't like about her.

"Trey?" Maddie lifted her head with a question in her eyes. "Did you go somewhere?"

Trey kissed her again, guiding her back down onto his bed. "Just regrouping," he said, realizing he'd lost his focus. He'd been in the middle of making love to a beautiful woman and bittersweet, niggling thoughts had crept into his head. He shoved them away and concentrated on Maddie and making her his, if only for tonight.

He slipped his hand down her torso, his fingers sliding under the red, lacy thong. He began stroking her softly.

"Mmmm, I like the way you regroup, *baby*."

Trey groaned. Maddie had a way with that one word that sent his heart racing and his body into overdrive. His strokes grew faster and she moved her body with more urgency, until Trey couldn't hold back another second. He knew the time was now. He reached for the bedside drawer and withdrew a condom. He'd picked them up shortly after their first time together, not trusting himself to keep his vow to stay away from her. At least that way, he'd act responsibly, if not rationally.

"Old ones?" Maddie asked, her brows lifting.

"New ones," he replied honestly, "with only your name on them." He handed one to her and she fitted it into place, taking her time and driving him crazy.

With a finger, he slipped her panties down her legs quickly. He came over her, parted her thighs and looked into her pretty green eyes. "I've missed you, Trey."

God, he'd missed her too.

He entered her in one careful thrust and Maddie cooed

softly.

Trey slammed his eyes shut, overwhelmed with the very same sentiment. The first time with her had been amazing, but this time their joining meant more than satisfying lust and desire. This time, it counted for more emotions than he could name.

As Trey drove his body deeper, he absorbed every sensation, every nuance that was Maddie, committing it to his memory. They moved together in sync, wrapped in each other's arms. And minutes later they climaxed in unison, their bodies joined, their heartbeats pulsing against each other.

He sank back to Earth, sated and complete. Trey took Maddie in his arms and held on tight, brushing his lips to her forehead, her cheeks. With each moment drawing closer to dawn, he feared he'd awaken an empty, hollow, defeated man.

TOO SOON MADDIE woke from a blissful, easy sleep. She opened her eyes to find Trey beside her, one arm draped protectively and provocatively below her waist. She smiled at the man she loved with her whole heart and reached up, not quite touching his face for fear of waking him. And that's how it was with Trey. Maddie had almost touched him, but she hadn't been able to get close enough to wake him out of his self-imposed sleep. She wanted to shake him and shout that he wasn't cursed, that he was a man she could count on, again and again.

But Trey had to decide that for himself. She knew that now. And she hoped that someday he'd come to that realization before it was too late.

Maddie rested her head against the pillow and sighed quietly. She'd be leaving him soon, the hour nearing dawn. But she took a minute to relive the night, recalling the way Trey made her feel when he touched her, recalling his hands on her body, making magic, creating tingles and shivers. So vividly, she recalled his lips on hers, the way he claimed her mouth with gentle command, forceful and demanding, but also sweet and tender.

He left no part of her untouched, making her feel treasured and loved. Having his hands on her body seemed as natural as breathing. There was no shame, no regret. Making love with him, having him inside her, felt like coming home.

Right as rain.

Good as gold.

He made her bold, when she'd never been before. He made her ache and then he soothed her. He made her wanton and then he satisfied her. He brought out her true self, the one she kept hidden from everyone else. Trey had filled her body, but he'd also filled her heart and her mind.

He'd done his best to push her away, yet she'd never felt closer to another human being. Her heart cried out for him in the worst way, but she knew that he had to come to terms with his past to gain his future.

Maddie sighed again, staring at Trey as he slept soundly. They'd made love twice last night, each time had been so different, so compelling, so *earth-shattering*.

A ray of predawn light entered the room—a dusky stream that appeared before the sun lifted high and bright in the sky. Maddie knew her time at 2 Hope was up. She rose from the bed and glanced at Trey one final time, her eyes growing wide, a barrier to her unshed tears.

She left his room.

She'd be off the ranch before dawn.

TREY PUNCHED OPEN the screen door and stepped onto the front porch. Sunlight beamed down and slapped him in the face, making him squint. "Damn it."

He'd overslept this morning for the first time in ten years. Deep, dark despair had washed over him, and it had been all he could do to drag himself out of bed today.

Maddie had left 2 Hope.

He'd been successful in his quest to drive her away.

And he hated himself for it.

Trey sat down on the bench seat and hung his head, thinking back on all the mistakes he'd made with her. Kissing her that first time had been his downfall. He'd known better than to get involved with wholesome, sweet Maddie Brooks. She was a keeper and he couldn't keep her.

God, how his head pounded.

"Headache, boss?" Kit asked, riding up on Julip.

More like heartache. "Nah, I'm fine. Taking her out for some exercise?"

Kit grinned and Trey wondered what the hell he was so happy about this time of the morning. "Something like that. Take a look-see."

Kit rode toward Storm's corral.

Trey stood and called out. "Hey, don't get her too close."

But his foreman pretended not to hear. He rode Julip closer to Storm. Immediately, Trey strode over, thinking Kit had lost his mind. "Careful!"

"Watch this," Kit said and continued until Julip was nose to nose with Storm, from opposite sides of the fence.

Trey reached the corral fence and stared at the two horses that were eyeing and sniffing each other like childhood sweethearts. He shot his foreman a curious look.

"That's not all," Kit said, still wearing that silly grin. Cued by Kit's soft clicking sound, Julip began to saunter around the perimeter of the corral at a moderate pace. And before Trey could blink his eyes, Storm joined in from his side of the fence, matching Julip stride for stride as if the two were out trotting on a Sunday excursion.

"I'll be damned."

Kit made three circles around and each time Julip allowed Storm to set the pace as the two horses moved together.

Kit returned with a triumphant smile on his face, Trey shook his head in disbelief. "How'd you do it?"

"Not me. Maddie. She asked me to continue working with Julip and Storm. It seems she found a way to settle your wild stallion without breaking his spirit."

This time, Trey did blink, three times, taking it all in. Maddie hadn't given up on Storm. Even though he'd confronted her, she never quit. He should have known. Maddie Brooks wasn't a quitter.

Storm came up to nudge Trey's hand. The stallion snorted in the air and shook his ink-black mane of hair. This was the first time Storm had approached him in a nonaggressive way. Trey reached up and stroked his mane, then patted his head with affection. "What a surprise."

"Nah, just nature taking its course, I'd say."

"Yeah," Trey replied, "maybe."

Trey couldn't get over Storm's transformation. Sure, he'd still have his moods—a stallion couldn't change that much—but he had changed enough to make him a true part of 2 Hope. Storm belonged here. He belonged to Trey. In a sense they belonged to each other.

"Then maybe you should let nature take its course in another way," Kit said.

Curious, Trey asked, "In what other way?"

Kit tipped his hat and smiled. "I was thinking that the

right woman could settle the right man. They'd be like soul mates. Sorta like what happened with Storm and Julip. It just takes some smarts to figure it all out, boss."

With that, Kit spurred Julip into a trot and they headed out. Trey stared at them as they rode off, his head still reeling. He walked over to the front steps and set himself down. Stretching out his legs, he thought about how wrong he'd been about his feisty stallion.

Maddie had been right.

Trey wondered what else he'd been wrong about lately, but he couldn't finish the thought because Jack pulled up to the house in his patrol car. He exited the car wearing a tight expression.

"Damn," he muttered. Jack was the last person he wanted to see today. "Nobody's home," Trey remarked, only halfway joking.

But Jack was never one to take a hint. He sat right down beside him and stared into his eyes. "You got that right." He pointed to Trey's head. "Nobody's home in there. Where's your head, Trey?"

"I'm not in the mood, Jack. Say what you came to say, or better yet, just leave."

"You're going to thank me one day for this," Jack said, all sarcasm gone. "Just keep it buttoned. I'm going to do some talking, and you're going to do some listening."

Trey humored him. "Okay, shoot."

"Just a sec." Jack walked into the house and came back

holding two beers. He set both down between them.

"It's nine o'clock in the morning."

Jack took his seat on the steps again. "You're gonna need it."

"I thought you were on duty."

Jack smiled. "They're both for you."

Trey grimaced and twisted the cap. "Okay, what?" Then he took a swig. Seemed a cold brew couldn't hurt. He already felt as though he'd been in a train wreck.

"I passed Maddie in town. Her truck was loaded up. She left the ranch, didn't she?"

Trey nodded, like he needed reminding.

"And you just let her go?"

He nodded again and stared at Jack defying him to make a snide comment.

Jack put up both hands in surrender. "I didn't come here to condemn you. I came here to reason with you."

Trey finished the first beer in two gulps then turned to his cousin. "Why?"

"Because any fool can see you're head over heels in love with her, that's why. And Lord only knows why, but Maddie feels the same way. I can't stand by and see you make that kind of mistake. You see, you've been holding onto this lame idea that you're like your father. But, Trey, let me clue you in, you're not the heartbreaker your daddy was. You haven't got a selfish bone in your body. And I know you're stuck on his dying words to you. But did you ever stop to think he didn't mean it that way?"

"*Don't make the same mistakes I made, son.* It's hard to misinterpret that," Trey said.

"Right, that's what he said. But maybe he meant that he wanted better for you. He didn't want you to be miserable and lonely without love in your life. It's possible that he knew you were capable of loving one woman and devoting your life to her. He knew he couldn't do that, but maybe he wanted to impress upon you that you could.

"Sure we bump heads from time to time, but I've got to tell you, I'm proud to call you my relation. Anybody can see what kind of man you are, Trey. And your father knew you through and through. I'd bet my last dollar that he never meant for you to lose someone as special as Maddie. I think he meant for you to find the right woman and *keep* her. You hit the jackpot, Trey. You found the right woman. You'd never hurt Maddie. I know that, and I think you know that, too. So *keep* her."

Trey's head cleared and suddenly, he saw the possibilities. Maybe his father had meant for him to have a better, more fulfilling life. Maybe he had believed Trey capable of love and devotion, something he couldn't quite manage. Maybe his father had thought Trey the better man. But could he look beyond his past and see instead a future with Maddie?

Hell, she'd been the one all along to believe in him even when he didn't believe in himself. She'd tried pointing out all the qualities she admired in him, tried to make him see he had worth and staying power. Maddie had faith enough for them both.

He slid his hand down his jaw, realizing he'd already hurt her in so many ways. He'd pushed her away again and again. He'd made love to her last night until they could barely move a muscle and then he'd let her leave the ranch. He'd made so many mistakes with her. "It's too late."

"No. She's not gone yet."

"She's not?" An inkling of hope developed.

"I saw her truck parked outside of the Cactus Inn."

"The Cactus Inn?"

"Hey, don't question it. Just consider it a lucky break. She's probably still there. I passed her not fifteen minutes ago."

Trey jumped up and gave Jack a big bear hug. "I owe you, cousin."

"Don't kiss me and we'll call it even. Now go."

Trey raced inside to grab his hat and keys and then headed out. He'd figure out what to say once he found her and prayed it would be enough.

TREY THANKED HIS lucky stars that Maddie's truck was still parked outside the Cactus Inn. He entered the motel and strode straight over to the reception desk. "Hi, Jody."

"Hey, Trey. Haven't seen you around much. What brings you in here?"

He and Trey had been buddies in high school and now Jody ran his late father's motel. "I'm looking for Dr. Brooks. You know, Maddie Brooks, the veterinarian."

Jody nodded. "Yeah, I know who she is. You're the third person to come looking for her this morning, and heck, she just checked in after breakfast."

"She checked *in?*"

Jody nodded.

"Who else came looking for her?"

Jody shrugged. "Don't know their names, but that woman sure has got herself a lot of gentlemen callers. First one, then another. Heck, Trey, you're the third this morning."

Trey grimaced, not knowing what to make of all this. There was only one way to find out. "What's her room number?"

"It's 202 D. Take the stairs then turn right. Boy, seems like I've said that a whole lot this morning."

"Thanks. Do you know if anyone is still up there?" Jody shrugged shoulders that had at one time blocked their high school football team's most competitive rivals. He'd been the best darn tackle at Hope Wells High. "Nope. Sorry, man. Good luck."

Puzzled, Trey climbed the stairs and found Maddie's room. He took in a lungful of air, still not sure what to say exactly and not even sure she'd be alone in there to listen. He knocked briskly. "Maddie, it's Trey."

Seconds ticked by. It seemed like a darn eternity. Then she opened the door and they stared into each other's eyes. Overwhelmed at seeing her again, at seeing what he might have lost, Trey's body shook powerfully, the tremble coursing the length of him.

Seeing her staring at him with curious green eyes, Trey realized just how much he loved this woman. He realized what a fool he'd been. He'd nearly tossed away the most precious thing that would ever enter his life. He stood there, gazing at her, seeing his future.

"Trey?"

Yanking off his Stetson, he smiled. "Morning."

She smiled back tentatively. Trey couldn't blame her. Basically, they'd said their good-byes between the sheets last night, so he understood her bafflement. She probably thought she'd never see him again. That was his fault. All of it was his fault.

"Morning."

"Can I come in? Or are you, uh, busy?"

"I'm busy, but of course you can come in."

Trey entered the small, quaint room noticing Maddie's suitcase opened and half of her clothes put up in the closet area. Her other belongings were strewn about the room. Fortunately though, they were alone.

Trey let his gaze wander for only a second or two, before lifting his eyes back to her. He was almost afraid if he took his eyes off her for too long, she'd vanish and he already knew how it felt to have Maddie there one minute, then gone the next. He didn't want to experience that sensation ever again.

"What are you doing here?" she asked quietly.

"I was wrong about Storm."

Maddie blinked. "You came here to talk about Storm?"

God, this was so hard. He didn't want to make her crazy, but Trey had never been great with words. "Not really, but I thought you should know that you were right all along. He's... well, he's as amazing as you are."

Maddie continued to stare at him, her expression softening a little. "Thank you," she said with a small smile.

God, how he loved her. She looked so darn pretty today with her auburn hair pulled back into a ponytail. Wearing nothing special, just jeans and a blouse, the wholesome woman he'd made passionate love to last night, was more beautiful, more sexy, more... everything, than any woman he'd ever met. It stunned him how much he'd already missed her at the ranch. Trey cleared his throat. "What, uh, what are you doing here?"

"Me? I'm moving in for a while."

"I thought you needed to get to Denver right away?"

Maddie frowned and Trey realized how his comment might appear to her—as if he was eager to see her go. Hell, he really wasn't good at this.

"I'm not moving to Denver."

Stunned, Trey's heart did a somersault. "You're not?"

"No. I never was, Trey."

Trey stared at her. "Denver would have been a great opportunity, but it isn't for me. Hope Wells is my home. I realized that yesterday. I have great friends here, a good practice. I have everything I want." Then she glanced away. "Well, almost everything."

Trey kept silent and she went on. "Seems my party wasn't the only surprise I received yesterday. My insurance came through. I have enough funds to rebuild my office. I decided to take some time off to work on the design. I've already contacted an architect, and he's going to help me with my plans. I said good-bye to Nick this morning, too."

Maddie smiled warmly and her eyes sparkled. "You see, Trey Walker. You're not the only one around here with *staying power*."

Once again, Maddie had amazed him. He took a moment to recover from her bold assessment then grinned, agreeing with her. Finally. "Damn straight, I'm not. We both have *staying power*."

Maddie let out an uncertain chuckle. "We do?"

He nodded. "Yeah, honey, we do. I just sort of figured it all out. I love you, Maddie. I love you so much that I can barely breathe. I love you so much that if you'd gone to Denver, I would have followed you and begged you to come back with me. And it took me all this time to realize it. No, that's not right. *You* made me realize it. You taught me so much. You had the trust and faith in me that I didn't have. You made me see myself in a different light. And if it's not too late—"

"Oh, Trey. It's not too late. It never could be." The guarded look on Maddie's face disappeared, replaced by a soft sweet expression. "I've always loved you."

Trey took her hand in his, weaving their fingers together and holding tight. "I know I've been a fool, but I'm ready to remedy that. I love you, sweetheart. I want to marry you and live the rest of my life with you by my side."

Maddie reached up to caress his cheek. "Yes."

Joyous, Trey flung his hat in the air. "Yes? Yes, you'll marry me?"

On tiptoes, Maddie kissed him soundly on the lips. "Yes. I'll marry you."

Staggered by his good fortune, Trey confessed. "I never thought I'd say those words."

Maddie agreed. "I never thought I'd *hear* those words."

Both laughed as Trey took her into his arms and kissed her long and hard, crushing their lips together. "Move back to the ranch. Live with me. Be my wife. Be my lover."

Maddie's beautiful face beamed. "I'll be all of those things to you, Trey. And more."

Trey couldn't keep from smiling, his heart soaring. "More?"

She nodded and led him over to the bed. "So much more, *baby*."

"I DO." TREY Walker uttered the words slowly, both awed and a little bit frightened. In a million lifetimes, he'd never dreamed he'd say those words. Especially not to Maddie Brooks, the auburn-haired beauty directly beside him, her wide eyes filled with love. They sat atop their mounts under an arbor of lush traveling vines in the small garden area behind his house at 2 Hope Ranch. Maddie insisted Storm be a part of the wedding, too, and the feisty yet gentled stallion carried the most beautiful bride Hope Wells had ever seen.

Trey took great pride in his soon-to-be wife. Maddie hadn't given up on Storm. She'd found a way, through patience, careful thought, and clever maneuvering, to bring the animal around. She'd read Storm correctly, bringing into his corral a gentle mare, one not impressed or intimidated by his wild nature. This was a female unlike all others and Storm, smart creature that he was, came to recognize that fact.

Trey smiled at the similarities, wondering if he wasn't actually marrying a sorceress. No, he realized instantly, the magic they made together was real and solid, not something that could be whirled away on a whim.

"I do, too," Maddie said, happy tears welling in her eyes. A gentle breeze blew by, messing her hair enough to give his down-home girl a sexy look.

Trey swallowed hard, intrigued by the young woman who'd be living with him until the end of time. In truth, the petite, green-eyed female scared the hell out of him with her innocent looks and wholesome demeanor. He'd never loved so deeply, so completely. Maddie was the exact sort of woman Trey wanted. And he planned to keep her in his heart forever.

Under the minister's guidance, Trey placed the ring on Maddie's finger and spoke his vows, peering deeply into her eyes and telling her in a silent message that she'd have no reason to ever doubt his love. His word is as good as gold.

Maddie smiled, sealing the deal with vows of her own.

Storm whinnied and sidled up against the mare that had settled him, brushing soft white satin against Trey's leg. He leaned over his saddle, lifted the delicate bridal veil and kissed his new wife.

The contract he'd just entered into with Maddie Brooks Walker was a marriage that had true staying power.

Just like 2 Hope Ranch, Storm and . . . *him.*

The End

You'll love the next book in the...
Forever Texan Series

Book 1: *Taming the Texas Cowboy*

Book 2: *Loving the Texas Lawman*
Coming soon

Book 3: *Redeeming the Texas Rancher*

More by Charlene Sands

Claim Me, Cowboy
Copper Mountain Rodeo series

Bachelor for Hire
Bachelor Auction Returns series

About the Author

Charlene Sands is a USA Today Bestselling author writing sexy contemporary romances and stories set in the Old West. Her stories have been honored with the National Readers Choice Award, the Cataromance Reviewer's Choice Award and she's a double recipient of the Booksellers' Best Award. She was recently honored with Romantic Times Magazine's Best Harlequin Desire of 2014. Charlene is a member of the Orange County Chapter and Los Angeles Chapter of Romance Writers of America.

When not writing, she enjoys great coffee, spending time with her four "princesses", bowling in a woman's league, country music, reading books from her favorite authors and going on movie dates with her "hero" husband.

Thank you for reading

Taming the Texas Cowboy

If you enjoyed this book, you can find more from all our great authors at TulePublishing.com, or from your favorite online retailer.

MAY 1 9 2017

Made in the USA
Lexington, KY
15 May 2017